WHO MIXED THE CYANIDE COCKTAIL?

It was certainly no way to celebrate Rosemary's birthday. On the other hand, each guest at the party had a motive for her murder.

Her husband, George Barton, resented the fact that his wife was all things to all men—except him. Her lover's promising political career would be over if their affair was discovered. Her lover's wife didn't care to lose her husband to Rosemary. Her husband's secretary wanted Mr. Barton, and only Mrs. Barton stood in her way. Her sister, Iris Marle, was penniless and sole heiress to Rosemary's fortune.

So a year later, on the same date, another party was held to trap the killer. Instead—DEATH STRUCK AGAIN!

REMEMBERED DEATH
was originally published by
Dodd, Mead & Company, Inc.

AGATHA CHRISTIE

REMEMBERED DEATH

(Original British title: Sparkling Cyanide)

PUBLISHED BY POCKET BOOKS NEW YORK

REMEMBERED DEATH

Dodd, Mead edition published 1945

POCKET BOOK edition published October, 1947

22nd printing....................December, 1975

L

This POCKET BOOK edition includes every word contained
in the original, higher-priced edition. It is printed from
brand-new plates made from completely reset, clear, easy-to-
read type. POCKET BOOK editions are published by POCKET
BOOKS, a division of Simon & Schuster, Inc., 630 Fifth
Avenue, New York, N.Y. 10020. Trademarks registered
in the United States and other countries.

CONTENTS

CAST OF CHARACTERS

REMEMBERED
DEATH

*Six people were thinking of
Rosemary Barton
who had died nearly a year ago . . .*

BOOK I

ROSEMARY

*"What can I do to drive away remembrance
from mine eyes?"*

CHAPTER 1   IRIS MARLE

I

IRIS MARLE was thinking about her sister, Rosemary.

For nearly a year she had deliberately tried to put the thought of Rosemary away from her. She hadn't wanted to remember.

It was too painful—too horrible!

The blue cyanosed face, the convulsed, clutching fingers . . .

The contrast between that and the gay lovely Rosemary of the day before . . . Well, perhaps not exactly *gay*. She had had "flu"—she had been depressed, run down . . . all that had been brought out at the inquest. Iris herself had laid stress on it. It accounted, didn't it, for Rosemary's suicide?

Once the inquest was over, Iris had deliberately tried to put the whole thing out of her mind. Of what good was remembrance? Forget it all! Forget the whole horrible business.

But now, she realized, she had got to remember. She had got to think back into the past . . . to remember carefully every slight unimportant seeming incident . . .

That extraordinary interview with George last night necessitated remembrance.

It had been so unexpected, so frightening. Wait—*had* it been so unexpected? Hadn't there been indications beforehand? George's growing absorption, his absent-mindedness, his unaccountable actions—his—well, *queerness* was the only word for it! All leading up to that moment last night when he had called her into the study and had taken the letters from the drawer of the desk.

So now there was no help for it. She had got to think about Rosemary—to *remember*.

Rosemary—her sister . . .

With a shock Iris realized suddenly that it was the first time in her life she had ever thought about Rosemary. Thought about her, that is, objectively as a *person*.

She had always accepted Rosemary without thinking about her. You didn't think about your mother or your father or your sister or your aunt. They just existed, unquestioned, in those relationships.

You didn't think about them as *people*. You didn't ask yourself, even, what they were *like*.

What had Rosemary been like?

That might be very important now. A lot might depend upon it. Iris cast her mind back into the past. Herself and Rosemary as children . . .

Rosemary had been the elder by six years.

Glimpses of the past came back—brief flashes—short scenes. Herself as a small child eating bread and milk, and Rosemary, important in pigtails, "doing lessons" at a table.

The seaside one summer—Iris envying Rosemary who was a "big girl" and could swim!

Rosemary going to boarding school—coming home for the holidays. Then she herself at school, and Rosemary being "finished" in Paris. Schoolgirl Rosemary—clumsy, all arms and legs. "Finished" Rosemary coming back from Paris with a strange new frightening elegance, soft-voiced, graceful, with a swaying, undulating figure, with red-gold chestnut hair and big, black-fringed, dark blue eyes. A disturbing, beautiful creature—grown up—in a different world!

From then on they had seen very little of each other, the six-year gap had been at its widest.

Iris had been still at school, Rosemary in the full swing of a "season." Even when Iris came home, the gap remained. Rosemary's life was one of late mornings in bed, fork luncheons with other débutantes, dances most evenings of the week. Iris had been in the schoolroom with Mademoiselle, had gone for walks in the park, had had supper at nine o'clock and had gone to bed at ten.

The intercourse between the sisters had been limited to such brief interchanges as:

"Hullo, Iris, telephone for a taxi for me, there's a lamb; I'm going to be devastatingly late," or "I don't like that new frock, Rosemary. It doesn't suit you. It's all bunch and fuss."

Then had come Rosemary's engagement to George Barton. Excitement, shopping, streams of parcels, bridesmaids' dresses.

The wedding. Walking up the aisle behind Rosemary, hearing whispers:

"What a *beautiful* bride she makes . . ."

Why had Rosemary married George? Even at the time Iris had been vaguely surprised. There had been so many exciting young men, ringing Rosemary up, taking her out. Why choose George Barton, fifteen years older than herself, kindly, pleasant, but definitely dull.

George was well off, but it wasn't money. Rosemary had her own money, a great deal of it.

Uncle Paul's money . . .

Irish searched her mind carefully, seeking to differentiate between what she knew now and what she had known then. Uncle Paul, for instance?

He wasn't really an uncle, she had always known that. Without ever having been definitely told them, she knew certain facts. Paul Bennett had been in love with her mother. She had preferred another and a poorer man. Paul Bennett had taken his defeat in a romantic spirit. He had remained the family friend, adopted an attitude of romantic, platonic devotion. He had become Uncle Paul, had stood godfather to the first-born child, Rosemary. When he died, it was found that he had left his

3

entire fortune to his little goddaughter, then a child of thirteen.

Rosemary, besides her beauty, had been an heiress. And she had married nice dull George Barton.

Why? Iris had wondered then. She wondered now. Iris didn't believe that Rosemary had ever been in love with him. But she had seemed very happy with him and she had been fond of him—yes, definitely fond of him. Iris had good opportunities for knowing, for a year after the marriage, their mother—lovely, delicate Viola Marle—had died, and Iris, a girl of seventeen, had gone to live with Rosemary Barton and her husband.

A girl of seventeen. Iris pondered over the picture of herself. What had she been like? What had she felt, thought, seen?

She came to the conclusion that that young Iris Marle had been slow of development—unthinking, acquiescing in things as they were. Had she resented, for instance, her mother's earlier absorption in Rosemary? On the whole she thought not. She had accepted, unhesitatingly, the fact that Rosemary was the important one. Rosemary was "out"—naturally her mother was occupied as far as her health permitted with her elder daughter. That had been natural enough. Her own turn would come some day. Viola Marle had always been a somewhat remote mother, preoccupied mainly with her own health, relegating her children to nurses, governesses, schools, but invariably charming to them in those brief moments when she came across them. Hector Marle had died when Iris was five years old. The knowledge that he drank more than was good for him had permeated so subtly that she had not the least idea how it had actually come to her.

Seventeen-year-old Iris Marle had accepted life as it came, had duly mourned for her mother, had worn black clothes, had gone to live with her sister and her sister's husband at their house in Elvaston Square.

Sometimes it had been rather dull in that house. Iris wasn't to come out, officially, until the following year. In the meantime, she took French and German lessons three times a week, and also attended domestic science classes. There were times when she had nothing much to do and

4

nobody to talk to. George was kind, invariably affectionate and brotherly. His attitude had never varied. He was
the same now.

And Rosemary? Iris had seen very little of Rosemary.
Rosemary had been out a good deal. Dressmakers, cocktail parties, bridge . . .

What did she really *know* about Rosemary when she
came to think of it? Of her tastes, of her hopes, of her
fears? Frightening, really, how little you might know of
a person after living in the same house with them! There
had been little or no intimacy between the sisters.

But she'd got to think now. She'd got to remember. It
might be important.

Certainly Rosemary had *seemed* happy enough . . .

Until that day—a week before it happened.

She, Iris, would never forget that day. It stood out
crystal clear—each detail, each word. The shining mahogany table, the pushed back chair, the hurried characteristic writing . . .

Iris closed her eyes and let the scene come back . . .

Her own entry into Rosemary's sitting room, her sudden stop.

It had startled her so, what she saw! Rosemary, sitting
at the writing table, her head laid down on her out-
stretched arms. Rosemary weeping with deep, abandoned
sobbing. She'd never seen Rosemary cry before—and this
bitter, violent weeping frightened her.

True, Rosemary had had a bad go of "flu." She'd only
been up a day or two. And everyone knew that "flu" *did*
leave you depressed. Still . . .

Iris had cried out, her voice childish, startled, "Oh,
Rosemary, what is it?"

Rosemary sat up, swept the hair back from her dis-
figured face. She struggled to regain command of herself.
She said quickly, "It's nothing—nothing—don't stare at
me like that!"

She got up and, passing her sister, ran out of the room.

Puzzled, upset, Iris went further into the room. Her
eyes, drawn wonderingly to the writing table, caught

sight of her own name in her sister's handwriting. Had Rosemary been writing to her then?

She drew nearer, looked down on the sheet of blue note-paper with the big, characteristic, sprawling writing, even more sprawling than usual owing to the haste and agitation behind the hand that held the pen.

Darling Iris,

There isn't any point in my making a will because my money goes to you anyway, but I'd like certain of my things to be given to certain people.

To George, the jewelry he's given me, and the little enamel casket we bought together when we were engaged.

To Gloria King, my platinum cigarette case.

To Maisie, my Chinese pottery horse that she's always admir—

It stopped there, with a frantic scrawl of the pen as Rosemary had dashed it down and given way to uncontrollable weeping.

Iris stood as though turned to stone.

What did it mean? Rosemary wasn't going to *die*, was she? She'd been very ill with influenza, but she was all right now. And anyway people didn't die of "flu"—at least sometimes they did, but Rosemary hadn't. She was quite well now, only weak and run down.

Iris's eyes went over the words again and this time a phrase stood out with startling effect. *My money goes to you anyway . . .*

It was the first intimation she had of the terms of Paul Bennett's will. She had known since she was a child that Rosemary had inherited Uncle Paul's money, that Rosemary was rich whilst she herself was comparatively poor. But until this moment she had never questioned what would happen to that money on Rosemary's death.

If she had been asked, she would have replied that she supposed it would go to George as Rosemary's husband, but would have added that it seemed absurd to think of Rosemary dying before George!

But here it was, set down in black and white, in Rosemary's own hand. At Rosemary's death the money came to her, Iris. But surely that wasn't legal? A husband or wife got any money that was left; not a *sister*. Unless, of course, Paul Bennett had left it that way in his will. Yes, that must be it. Uncle Paul had said the money was to go to her if Rosemary died. That did make it rather less unfair . . .

Unfair? She was startled as the word leaped to her thoughts. Had she then been thinking it was unfair for Rosemary to get *all* of Uncle Paul's money? She supposed that, deep down, she must have been feeling just that. It *was* unfair. They were sisters, she and Rosemary. They were both her mother's children. Why should Uncle Paul give it all to Rosemary?

Rosemary had always had everything!

Parties and frocks, and young men in love with her, and an adoring husband.

The only unpleasant thing that had ever happened to Rosemary was having an attack of "flu!" And even *that* hadn't lasted longer than a week!

Iris hesitated, standing by the desk. That sheet of paper —would Rosemary want it left about for the servants to see?

After a minute's hesitation she picked it up, folded it in two and slipped it into one of the drawers of the desk.

It was found there after the fatal birthday party, and provided an additional proof, if proof were necessary, that Rosemary had been in a depressed and unhappy state of mind after her illness, and had possibly been thinking of suicide even then.

Depression after influenza. That was the motive brought forward at the inquest, the motive that Iris's evidence helped to establish. An inadequate motive, perhaps, but the only one available, and consequently accepted. It had been a bad type of influenza that year.

Neither Iris nor George Barton could have suggested any other motive—*then*.

Now, thinking back over the incident in the attic afterward, Iris wondered that she could have been so blind.

The whole thing must have been going on under her eyes! And she had seen nothing, noticed nothing!

7

Her mind took a quick leap over the tragedy of the birthday party. No need to think of *that!* That was over —done with. Put away the horror of that and the inquest and George's twitching face and bloodshot eyes. Go straight on to the incident of the trunk in the attic.

II

That had been about six months after Rosemary's death.

Iris had continued to live at the house in Elvaston Square. After the funeral the Marle family solicitor, a courtly old gentleman with a shining bald head and unexpectedly shrewd eyes, had had an interview with Iris. He had explained with admirable clarity that under the will of Paul Bennett, Rosemary had inherited his estate in trust to pass, at her death, to any children she might have. If Rosemary died childless, the estate was to go to Iris absolutely. It was, the solicitor explained, a very large fortune which would belong to her absolutely upon attaining the age of twenty-one or on her marriage.

In the meantime, the first thing to settle was her place of residence. Mr. George Barton had shown himself anxious for her to continue living with him and had suggested that her father's sister, Mrs. Drake, who was in impoverished circumstances owing to the financial claims of a son (the black sheep of the Marle family), should make her home with them and chaperon Iris in society. Did Iris approve of this plan?

Iris had been quite willing, thankful not to have to make new plans. Aunt Lucilla she remembered as an amiable, elderly sheep with little will of her own.

So the matter had been settled. George Barton had been touchingly pleased to have his wife's sister still with him and treated her affectionately as a younger sister. Mrs. Drake, if not a stimulating companion, was completely subservient to Iris's wishes. The household settled down amicably.

It was nearly six months later that Iris made her discovery in the attic.

The attics of the Elvaston Square house were used as

storage rooms for odds and ends of furniture, and a number of trunks and suit-cases.

Iris had gone up there one day after an unsuccessful hunt for an old red pullover for which she had an affection. George had begged her not to wear mourning for Rosemary. Rosemary had always been opposed to the idea, he said. This, Iris knew, was true, so she acquiesced and continued to wear ordinary clothes, somewhat to the disapproval of Lucilla Drake who was old-fashioned and liked what she called "the decencies" to be observed. Mrs. Drake herself was still inclined to wear crêpe for a husband deceased some twenty-odd years ago!

Various unwanted clothes, Iris knew, had been packed away in a trunk upstairs. She started hunting through it for her pullover, coming across, as she did so, various forgotten belongings—a grey coat and skirt, a pile of stockings, her skiing kit and one or two old bathing suits.

It was then that she came across an old dressing-gown that had belonged to Rosemary and which had somehow or other escaped being given away with the rest of Rosemary's things. It was a mannish affair of spotted silk with big pockets.

Iris shook it out, nothing that it was in perfectly good condition. Then she folded it carefully and returned it to the trunk. As she did so, her hand felt something crackle in one of the pockets. She thrust in her hand and drew out a crumpled-up piece of paper. It was in Rosemary's handwriting and she smoothed it out and read it.

Leopard darling, you can't mean it . . . You can't —you can't . . . We love each other! We belong together! You must know that just as I know it! We can't just say good-bye and go on coolly with our own lives. You know that's impossible, darling—quite impossible. You and I belong together—forever and ever. I'm not a conventional woman—I don't mind what people say. Love matters more to me than anything else. We'll go away together—and be happy— I'll make you happy. You said to me once that life without me was dust and ashes to you—do you remember, Leopard, darling? And now you write calm-

ly that all this had better end—that it's only fair to me. Fair to me? But I can't live without you! I'm sorry about George—he's always been sweet to me —but he'll understand. He'll want to give me my freedom. It isn't right to live together if you don't love each other any more. God meant us for each other, darling—I know He did. We're going to be wonderfully happy—but we must be brave. I shall tell George myself—I want to be quite straight about the whole thing—but not until after my birthday.

I know I'm doing what's right, Leopard darling— and I can't live without you—can't—can't—CAN'T. How stupid it is of me to write all this. Two lines would have done. Just "I love you. I'm never going to let you go." Oh, darling—

The letter broke off.

Iris stood motionless, staring down at it. How little one knew of one's own sister!

So Rosemary had had a lover—had written him passionate love letters—had planned to go away with him?

What had happened? Rosemary had never sent the letter after all. What letter had she sent? What had finally been decided between Rosemary and this unknown man? ("Leopard!" What extraordinary fancies people had when they were in love. So silly. *Leopard* indeed!)

Who was this man? Did he love Rosemary as much as she loved him? Surely he must have. Rosemary was so unbelievably lovely. And yet, according to Rosemary's letter, he had suggested "ending it all." That suggested— what? Caution? He had evidently said that the break was for Rosemary's sake. That it was only fair to her. Yes, but didn't men say that sort of thing to save their faces? Didn't it really mean that the man, whoever he was, was tired of it all? Perhaps it had been to him a mere passing distraction. Perhaps he had never really cared. Somehow Iris got the impression that that unknown man had been very determined to break with Rosemary finally.

But Rosemary had thought differently. Rosemary wasn't going to count the cost. She had been determined, too.

Iris shivered.

And she, Iris, hadn't known a thing about it! Hadn't even guessed! Had taken it for granted that Rosemary was happy and contented and that she and George were quite satisfied with one another. Blind! She must have been blind not to know a thing like that about her own sister.

But who was the man?

She cast her mind back, thinking, remembering. There had been so many men about, admiring Rosemary, taking her out, ringing her up. There had been no one special. But there must have been—the rest of the bunch were mere camouflage for the one, the only one, who mattered. Iris frowned perplexedly, sorting her remembrances carefully.

Two names stood out: It must, yes, positively it must, be one or the other. Stephen Farraday? It must be Stephen Farraday. What could Rosemary have seen in him? A stiff, pompous young man—and not so very young either. Of course, people did say he was brilliant. A rising politician, an under-secretaryship prophesied in the near future, and all the weight of the influential Kidderminster connection behind him. A possible future Prime Minister! Was that what had given him glamour in Rosemary's eyes? Surely she couldn't care so desperately for the man himself—such a cold, self-contained creature? But they said that his own wife was passionately in love with him, that she had gone against all the wishes of her powerful family in marrying him—a mere nobody with political ambitions! If one woman felt like that about him, another woman might also. Yes, it *must* be Stephen Farraday.

Because, if it wasn't Stephen Farraday, it must be Anthony Browne.

And Iris didn't want it to be Anthony Browne.

True, he'd been very much Rosemary's slave, constantly at her beck and call, his dark, good-looking face expressing a kind of humorous desperation. But surely that devotion had been too open, too freely declared to go really deep.

Odd the way he had disappeared after Rosemary's death. They had none of them seen him since.

Still not so odd, really—he was a man who travelled a lot. He had talked about the Argentine and Canada and Uganda and the U.S.A. Iris had an idea that he was actually an American or a Canadian, though he had hardly any accent. No, it wasn't really strange that they shouldn't have seen anything of him since.

It was Rosemary who had been his friend. There was no reason why he should go on coming to see the rest of them. He had been Rosemary's friend. But not Rosemary's lover! Iris didn't want him to have been Rosemary's lover. That would hurt—that would hurt terribly.

She looked down at the letter in her hand. She crumpled it up. She'd throw it away, burn it . . .

It was sheer instinct that stopped her.

Some day it might be important to produce that letter . . .

She smoothed it out, took it down with her and locked it away in her jewel case.

It might be important, some day, to show why Rosemary took her own life.

III

"And the next thing, please?"

The ridiculous phrase came unbidden into Iris's mind and twisted her lips in a wry smile. The glib shopkeeper's question seemed to represent so exactly her own carefully directed mental processes.

Was not that exactly what she was trying to do in her survey of the past? She had dealt with the surprising discovery in the attic. And now—on to "the next thing, please!" What was the next thing?

Surely, the increasingly odd behaviour of George. That dated back for a long time. Little things that had puzzled her became clear now in the light of the surprising interview last night. Disconnected remarks and actions took their proper places in the course of events.

And there was the reappearance of Anthony Browne. Yes, perhaps that ought to come next in sequence, since it had followed the finding of the letter by just one week.

Iris could recall her sensations exactly . . .

Rosemary had died in November. In the following May, Iris, under the wing of Lucilla Drake, had started her social young girl's life. She had gone to luncheons and teas and dances without, however, enjoying them very much. She had felt listless and unsatisfied. It was at a somewhat dull dance towards the end of June that she heard a voice say behind her, "It *is* Iris Marle, isn't it?"

She had turned, flushing, to look into Anthony's—Tony's—dark quizzical face.

He said, "I don't expect you remember me, but—"

She interrupted.

"Oh, but I do remember you. Of course I do!"

"Splendid. I was afraid you'd have forgotten me. It's such a long time since I saw you."

"I know. Not since Rosemary's birthday par—"

She stopped. The words came gaily, unthinkingly, to her lips. Now the colour rushed away from her cheeks, leaving them white and drained of blood. Her lips quivered. Her eyes were suddenly wide and dismayed.

Anthony Browne said quickly, "I'm terribly sorry. I'm a brute to have reminded you."

Iris swallowed. She said, "It's all right."

(Not since the night of Rosemary's birthday party. Not since the night of Rosemary's suicide. She wouldn't think of it. She would *not* think of it!)

Anthony Browne said again, "I'm terribly sorry. Please forgive me. Shall we dance?"

She nodded. Although already engaged for the dance that was just beginning, she had floated onto the floor in his arms. She saw her partner, a blushing immature young man whose collar seemed too big for him, peering about for her. The sort of partner, she thought scornfully, that debs have to put up with. Not like this man—Rosemary's friend.

A sharp pang went through her. *Rosemary's friend.* That letter. Had it been written to this man she was dancing with now? Something in the easy feline grace with which he danced lent substance to the nickname "Leopard." Had he and Rosemary—

She said sharply, "Where have you been all this time?"

13

He held her a little away from him, looking down into her face. He was unsmiling now, his voice held coldness.

"I've been travelling—on business."

"I see." She went on uncontrollably: "Why have you come back?"

He smiled then. He said lightly, "Perhaps—to see you, Iris Marle."

And suddenly gathering her up a little closer, he executed a long daring glide through the dancers, a miracle of timing and steering. Iris wondered why, with a sensation that was almost wholly pleasure, she should feel afraid.

Since then Anthony had definitely become part of her life. She saw him at least once a week.

She met him in the park, at various dances, found him put next to her at dinner.

The only place he never came to was the house in Elvaston Square. It was some time before she noticed this, so adroitly did he manage to evade or refuse invitations there. When she did realize it she began to wonder why. Was it because he and Rosemary—

Then, to her astonishment, George—easy-going, non-interfering George—spoke to her about him.

"Who's this fellow, Anthony Browne, you're going about with? What do you know about him?"

She stared at him.

"Know about him? Why, he was a friend of Rosemary's!"

George's face twitched. He blinked. He said in a dull, heavy voice, "Yes, of course; so he was."

Iris cried remorsefully, "I'm sorry. I shouldn't have reminded you."

George Barton shook his head. He said gently, "No, no, I don't want her forgotten. Never that. After all," he spoke awkwardly, his eyes averted, "that's what her name means. Rosemary—remembrance." He looked full at her. "I don't want you to forget your sister, Iris."

She caught her breath.

"I never shall."

George went on. "But about this young fellow, Anthony Browne. Rosemary may have liked him, but I don't believe

14

she knew much about him. You know, you've got to be careful, Iris. You're a very rich young woman."

A kind of burning anger swept over her.

"Tony—Anthony—has plenty of money himself. Why, he stays at Claridge's when he's in London."

George Barton smiled a little. He murmured, "Eminently respectable—as well as costly. All the same, my dear, nobody seems to know much about the fellow."

"He's an American."

"Perhaps. If so, it's odd he isn't sponsored more by his own Embassy. He doesn't come much to this house, does he?"

"No. And I can see why, if you're so horrid about him!"

George shook his head.

"Seem to have put my foot in it. Oh, well. Only wanted to give you a timely warning. I'll have a word with Lucilla."

"Lucilla!" said Iris scornfully.

George said anxiously, "Is everything all right? I mean, does Lucilla see to it that you get the sort of time you ought to have? Parties—all that sort of thing?"

"Yes, indeed, she works like a beaver . . ."

"Because, if not, you've only got to say so, you know, child. We could get hold of someone else. Someone younger and more up to date. I want you to enjoy yourself."

"I do, George. Oh, George, I do."

He said rather heavily, "Then that's all right. I'm not much of a hand at these shows myself—never was. But see to it you get everything you want. There's no need to stint expense."

That was George all over—kind, awkward, blundering.

True to his promise, or threat, he "had a word" with Mrs. Drake on the subject of Anthony Browne, but as Fate would have it the moment was unpropitious for gaining Lucilla's full attention.

She had just had a cable from that ne'er-do-well son who was the apple of her eye and who knew, only too well, how to wring the maternal heart-strings to his own financial advantage.

"CAN YOU SEND ME TWO HUNDRED POUNDS? DESPER-
ATE. LIFE OR DEATH. VICTOR."

Lucilla was crying.

"Victor is so honourable. He knows how straitened my
circumstances are and he'd never apply to me except in
the last resource. He never has. I'm always so afraid he'll
shoot himself."

"Not he," said George Barton unfeelingly.

"You don't know him. I'm his mother and naturally I
know what my own son is like. I should never forgive myself if I didn't do what he asked. I could manage by selling out those shares."

George sighed.

"Look here, Lucilla. I'll get full information by cable
from one of my correspondents out there. We'll find out
just exactly what sort of a jam Victor's in. But my advice
to you is to let him stew in his own juice. He'll never
make good until you do."

"You're so hard, George. The poor boy has always
been unlucky—"

George repressed his opinions on that point. Never any
good arguing with women.

He merely said, "I'll get Ruth on to it at once. We
should hear by to-morrow."

Lucilla was partially appeased. The two hundred was
eventually cut down to fifty, but that amount Lucilla
firmly insisted on sending.

George, Iris knew, provided the amount himself though
pretending to Lucilla that he was selling her shares. Iris
admired George very much for his generosity and said
so. His answer was simple.

"Way I look at it—always some black sheep in the
family. Always someone who's got to be kept. Someone or
other will have to fork out for Victor until he dies."

"But it needn't be you. He's not *your* family."

"Rosemary's family is *mine.*"

"You're a darling, George. But couldn't *I* do it? You're
always telling me I'm rolling."

He grinned at her.

"Can't do anything of that kind until you're twenty-one,

16

young woman. And if you're wise you won't do it then. But I'll give you one tip. When a fellow wires that he'll end everything unless he gets a couple of hundred by return, you'll usually find that twenty pounds will be ample . . . I daresay a tenner would do! You can't stop a mother coughing up, but you can reduce the amount—remember that. Of course, Victor Drake would never do away with himself, not he! These people who threaten suicide never do it."

Never? Iris thought of Rosemary. Then she pushed the thought away. George wasn't thinking of Rosemary. He was thinking of an unscrupulous, plausible young man in Rio de Janeiro .

The net gain from Iris's point of view was that Lucilla's maternal preoccupations kept her from paying full attention to Iris's friendship with Anthony Browne.

So—on to the "next thing, Madam." The change in George! Iris couldn't put it off any longer. When had that begun? What was the cause of it?

Even now, thinking back, Iris could not put her finger definitely on the moment when it began. Ever since Rosemary's death George had been abstracted, had had fits of inattention and brooding. He had seemed older, heavier. That was all natural enough. But when exactly had his abstraction become something more than natural?

It was, she thought, after their clash over Anthony Browne, that she had first noticed him staring at her in a bemused, perplexed manner. Then he formed a new habit of coming home early from business and shutting himself up in his study. He didn't seem to be doing anything in there. She had gone in once and found him sitting at his desk staring straight ahead of him. He looked at her when she came in with dull, lack-lustre eyes. He behaved like a man who has had a shock, but to her question as to what was the matter, he replied briefly, "Nothing."

As the days passed, he went about with the careworn look of a man who has some definite worry upon his mind.

17

Nobody had paid very much attention. Iris certainly hadn't. Worries were always conveniently "business."

Then, at odd intervals, and with no seeming reason, he began to ask questions. It was then that she began to put his manner down as definitely "queer."

"Look here, Iris, did Rosemary ever talk to you much?" Iris stared at him.

"Why, of course, George. At least—well, what about?"

"Oh, herself—her friends—how things were going with her. Whether she was happy or unhappy. That sort of thing."

She thought she saw what was in his mind. He must have got wind of Rosemary's unhappy love affair.

She said slowly, "She never said much. I mean—she was always busy—doing things."

"And you were only a kid, of course. Yes, I know. All the same, I thought she might have said something."

He looked at her inquiringly—rather like a hopeful dog. She didn't want George to be hurt. And anyway Rosemary never *had* said anything. She shook her head.

George sighed. He said heavily, "Oh, well, it doesn't matter."

Another day he asked her suddenly who Rosemary's best women friends had been.

Iris reflected.

"Gloria King. Mrs. Atwell—Maisie Atwell. Jean Raymond."

"How intimate was she with them?"

"Well, I don't know exactly."

"I mean, do you think she might have confided in any of them?"

"I don't really know . . . I don't think it's awfully likely . . . What sort of confiding do you mean?"

Immediately she wished she hadn't asked that last question, but George's response to it surprised her.

"Did Rosemary ever say she was afraid of anybody?"

"Afraid?" Iris stared.

"What I'm trying to get at is, did Rosemary have any enemies?"

"Amongst other women?"

"No, no, not that kind of thing. Real enemies. There

18

wasn't anyone—that you knew of—who—who might have had it in for her?"

Iris's frank stare seemed to upset him. He reddened, muttered, "Sounds silly, I know. Melodramatic, but I just wondered."

It was a day or two after that that he started asking about the Farradays.

How much had Rosemary seen of the Farradays?

Iris was doubtful.

"I don't really know, George."

"Did she ever talk about them?"

"No, I don't think so."

"Were they intimate at all?"

"Rosemary was very interested in politics."

"Yes. After she met the Farradays in Switzerland. Never cared a button about politics before that."

"No. I think Stephen Farraday interested her in them. He used to lend her pamphlets and things."

George said, "What did Sandra Farraday think about it?"

"About what?"

"About her husband lending Rosemary pamphlets."

Iris said uncomfortably, "I don't know."

George said, "She's a very reserved woman. Looks cold as ice. But they say she's crazy about Farraday. Sort of woman who might resent his having a friendship with another woman."

"Perhaps."

"How did Rosemary and Farraday's wife get on?"

Iris said slowly, "I don't think they did. Rosemary laughed at Sandra. Said she was one of those stuffed political women like a rocking-horse. (She is rather like a horse, you know.) Rosemary used to say that 'if you pricked her sawdust would ooze out.' "

George grunted. Then he said, "Still seeing a good deal of Anthony Browne?"

"A fair amount." Iris's voice was cold, but George did not repeat his warnings. Instead he seemed interested.

"Knocked about a good deal, hasn't he? Must have had an interesting life. Does he ever talk to you about it?"

"Not much. He's travelled a lot, of course."

"Business, I suppose."

"I suppose so."

"What is his business?"

"I don't know."

"Something to do with armament firms, isn't it?"

"He's never said."

"Well, needn't mention I asked. I just wondered. He was about a lot last Autumn with Dewsbury who's the chairman of United Arms Ltd. . . . Rosemary saw rather a lot of Anthony Browne, didn't she?"

"Yes—yes, she did."

"But she hadn't know him very long—he was more or less of a casual acquaintance. Used to take her dancing, didn't he?"

"Yes."

"I was rather surprised, you know, that she wanted him at her birthday party. Didn't realize she knew him so well."

Iris said quietly, "He dances very well."

"Yes—yes, of course."

Without wishing to, Iris unwillingly let a picture of that evening flit across her mind.

The round table at the Luxembourg, the shaded lights, the flowers. The dance band with its insistent rhythm. The seven people around the table: herself, Anthony Browne, Rosemary, Stephen Farraday, Ruth Lessing, George, and on George's right, Stephen Farraday's wife, Lady Alexandra Farraday, with her pale straight hair and those slightly arched nostrils and her clear arrogant voice. Such a gay party it had been—or hadn't it?

And in the middle of it, Rosemary—*no, no, better not think about that.* Better only to remember herself sitting next to Tony—that was the first time she had really met him. Before that he had been only a name, a shadow in the hall, a back accompanying Rosemary down the steps in front of the house to a waiting taxi.

Tony—

She came back with a start. George was repeating a question.

"Funny he cleared off so soon after. Where did he go, do you know?"

She said vaguely, "Oh, Ceylon, I think, or India."

"Never mentioned it that night."

Iris said sharply, "Why should he? And have we got to talk about—that night?"

His face crimsoned over.

"No, no, of course not. Sorry, old thing. By the way, ask Browne to dinner one night. I'd like to meet him again."

Iris was delighted. George was coming round. The invitation was duly given and accepted, but at the last minute Anthony had to go north on business and couldn't come.

One day at the end of July, George startled both Lucilla and Iris by announcing that he had bought a house in the country.

"Bought a *house?*" Iris was incredulous. "But I thought we were going to rent that house at Goring for two months?"

"Nicer to have a place of one's own—eh? Can go down for week-ends all through the year."

"Where it is? On the river?"

"Not exactly. In fact, not at all. Sussex. Marlingham. Little Priors, it's called. Twelve acres—small Georgian house."

"Do you mean you've bought it without us even seeing it?"

"Rather a chance. Just came into the market. Snapped it up."

Mrs. Drake said, "I suppose it will need a lot of doing up and redecorating."

George said in an off-hand way, "Oh, that's all right. Ruth has seen to all that."

They received the mention of Ruth Lessing, George's capable secretary, in respectful silence. Ruth was an institution—practically one of the family. Good-looking in a severe black and white kind of way, she was the essence of efficiency combined with tact . . .

During Rosemary's lifetime, it had been usual for Rosemary to say, "Let's get Ruth to see to it. She's marvellous. Oh, leave it to Ruth."

Every difficulty could always be smoothed out by Miss

Lessing's capable fingers. Smiling, pleasant, aloof, she surmounted all obstacles. She ran George's office and, it was suspected, ran George as well. He was devoted to her and leaned upon her judgment in every way. She seemed to have no needs, no desires of her own.

Nevertheless, on this occasion Lucilla Drake was annoyed.

"My dear George, capable as Ruth is, well, I mean— the women of a family do like to arrange the colour scheme of their own drawing-room! Iris should have been consulted. I say nothing about myself. *I* do not count. But it is annoying for Iris."

George looked conscience-stricken.

"I wanted it to be a surprise!"

Lucilla had to smile.

"What a boy you are, George."

Iris said, "I don't mind about colour schemes. I'm sure Ruth will have made it perfect. She's so clever. What shall we do down there? There's a tennis court, I suppose."

"Yes, and golf links six miles away, and it's only about fourteen miles to the sea. What's more, we shall have neighbours. Always wise to go to a part of the world where you know somebody, I think."

"What neighbours?" asked Iris sharply.

George did not meet her eyes.

"The Farradays," he said. "They live about a mile and a half away just across the park."

Iris stared at him. In a minute she leaped to the conviction that the whole of this elaborate business, the purchasing and equipping of a country house, had been undertaken with one object only—to bring George into close relationship with Stephen and Sandra Farraday. Near neighbours in the country, with adjoining estates, the two families were bound to be on intimate terms. Either that or a deliberate coolness!

But why? Why this persistent harping on the Farradays? Why this costly method of achieving an incomprehensible aim?

Did George suspect that Rosemary and Stephen Farraday had been something more than friends? Was this a strange manifestation of post-mortem jealousy? Surely that was a thought too far-fetched for words!

But what *did* George want from the Farradays? What was the point of all the odd questions he was continually shooting at her, Iris? Wasn't there something very queer about George lately?

The odd fuddled look he had in the evenings! Lucilla attributed it to a glass or so too much of port. Lucilla would!

No, there was something queer about George lately. He seemed to be labouring under a mixture of excitement intrelarded with great spaces of complete apathy when he sat sunk in a coma.

Most of that August they spent in the country at Little Priors. Horrible house! Iris shivered. She hated it. A gracious, well-built house, harmoniously furnished and decorated. (Ruth Lessing was never at fault!) And curiously, frighteningly *vacant*. They didn't live there. They *occupied* it. As soldiers, in a war, occupied some lookout post.

What made it horrible was the overlay of ordinary, normal summer living. People down for week-ends, tennis parties, informal dinners with the Farradays. Sandra Farraday had been charming to them—the perfect manner to neighbours who were already friends. She introduced them to the county, advised George and Iris about horses, was prettily deferential to Lucilla as an older woman.

And behind the mask of her pale smiling face no one could know what she was thinking. A woman like a sphinx.

Of Stephen they had seen little. He was very busy, often absent on political business. To Iris it seemed certain that he deliberately avoided meeting the Little Priors party more than he could help.

So August had passed and September, and it was decided that in October they should go back to the London house.

Iris had drawn a deep breath of relief. Perhaps, once they were back George would return to his normal self.

And then, last night, she had been roused by a low tapping on her door. She switched on the light and glanced at the time. Only one o'clock. She had gone to bed at half past ten and it had seemed to her it was much later.

She threw on a dressing-gown and went to the door. Somehow that seemed more natural than just to shout "Come in."

George was standing outside. He had not been to bed and was still in his evening clothes. His breath was coming unevenly and his face was a curious blue colour.

He said, "Come down to the study, Iris. I've got to talk to you. I've got to talk to someone."

Wondering, still dazed with sleep, she obeyed.

Inside the study, he shut the door and motioned her to sit opposite him at the desk. He pushed the cigarette box across to her, at the same time taking one and lighting it, after one or two attempts, with a shaking hand.

She said, "Is anything the matter, George?"

She was really alarmed now. He looked ghastly.

George spoke between small gasps, like a man who has been running.

"I can't go on by myself. I can't keep it any longer. You've got to tell me what you think—whether it's true— whether it's *possible*—"

"But what is it you're talking about, George?"

"You must have noticed something, seen something. There must have been something she *said*. There must have been a *reason*—"

She stared at him.

He passed his hand over his forehead.

"You don't understand what I'm talking about. I can see that. Don't look so scared, little girl. You've got to help me. You've got to remember every damned thing you can. Now, now, I know I sound a bit incoherent, but you'll understand in a minute—when I've shown you the letters."

He unlocked one of the drawers at the side of the desk and took out two single sheets of paper.

They were of a pale innocuous blue, with words printed on them, small and primly.

"Read that," said George, handing her one sheet.

Iris stared down at the paper. What it said was quite clear and devoid of circumlocution:

24

YOU THINK YOUR WIFE COMMITTED SUICIDE. SHE DIDN'T. SHE WAS KILLED.

The second ran,

YOUR WIFE, ROSEMARY, DIDN'T KILL HERSELF. SHE WAS MURDERED.

As Iris stayed staring at the words, George went on.

"They came about three months ago. At first I thought it was a joke—a cruel, rotten sort of joke. Then I began to think. Why *should* Rosemary have killed herself?"

Iris said in a mechanical voice, "Depression after influenza."

"Yes, but really when you come to think of it, that's rather piffle, isn't it? I mean lots of people have influenza and feel a bit depressed afterwards—what?"

Iris said with an effort, "She might—have been unhappy?"

"Yes, I suppose she might." George considered the point quite calmly. "But all the same I don't see Rosemary putting an end to herself because she was unhappy. She might threaten to, but I don't think she would really do it when it came to the point."

"But she *must* have done so, George! What other explanation could there be? Why, they even found the stuff in her handbag."

"I know. It all hangs together. But ever since these came," he tapped the anonymous letters with his finger nail, "I've been turning things over in my mind. And the more I've thought about it the more I feel sure there's something in it. That's why I've asked you all those questions—about Rosemary ever making any enemies. About anything she'd ever said that sounded as thought she were afraid of someone. Whoever killed her must have had a *reason*—"

"But, George, you're crazy—"

"Sometimes I think I am. Other times I know that I'm on the right track. But I've got to *know*. I've got to find out. You've got to help me, Iris. You've got to *think*. You've got to remember. That's it—*remember*. Go back over that night again and again. Because you do see, don't you, that if she was killed, it *must have been some-*

25

one who was at the table that night? You do see that, don't you?"

Yes, she had seen that. There was no pushing aside the remembrance of that scene any longer. She must remember it all. The music, the roll of drums, the lowered lights, the cabaret and the lights going up again and Rosemary sprawled forward on the table, her face blue and convulsed.

Iris shivered. She was frightened now—horribly frightened . . .

She must think—go back—remember.

Rosemary, that's for remembrance.

There was to be no oblivion.

CHAPTER 2   RUTH LESSING

RUTH LESSING, during a momentary lull in her busy day, was remembering her employer's wife, Rosemary Barton.

She had disliked Rosemary Barton a good deal. She had never known quite how much until that November morning when she had first talked with Victor Drake.

That interview with Victor had been the beginning of it all, had set the whole train in motion. Before then, the things she had felt and thought had been so far below the stream of her consciousness that she hadn't really known about them.

She was devoted to George Barton. She always had been. When she had first come to him, a cool, competent young woman of twenty-three, she had seen that he needed taking charge of. She had taken charge of him. She had saved him time, money and worry. She had chosen his friends for him, and directed him to suitable hobbies. She had restrained him from ill-advised business adventures, and encouraged him to take judicious risks on occasions. Never once in their long association had George suspected her of being anything other than subservient, attentive, and entirely directed by himself. He took a

26

distinct pleasure in her appearance, the neat, shining dark head, the smart tailor-mades and crisp shirts, the small pearls in her well-shaped ears, the pale, discreetly powdered face, and the faint restrained rose shade of her lipstick.

Ruth, he felt, was absolutely right.

He liked her detached impersonal manner, her complete absence of sentiment or familiarity. In consequence he talked to her a good deal about his private affairs and she listened sympathetically and always put in a useful word of advice.

She had nothing to do, however, with his marriage. She did not like it. However, she accepted it and was invaluable in helping with the wedding arrangements, relieving Mrs. Marle of a great deal of work.

For a time after the marriage, Ruth was on slightly less confidential terms with her employer. She confined herself strictly to the office affairs. George left a good deal in her hands.

Nevertheless, such was her efficiency that Rosemary soon found that George's Miss Lessing was an invaluable aid in all sorts of ways. Miss Lessing was always pleasant, smiling and polite.

George, Rosemary and Iris all called her Ruth and she often came to Elvaston Square to lunch. She was now twenty-nine and looked exactly the same as she had looked at twenty-three.

Without an intimate word ever passing between them, she was always perfectly aware of George's slightest emotional reactions. She knew when the first elation of his married life passed into an ecstatic content, she was aware when that content gave way to something else that was not so easy to define. A certain inattention to details shown by him at this time was corrected by her own forethought.

However distrait George might be, Ruth Lessing never seemed to be aware of it. He was grateful to her for that.

It was on a November morning that he spoke to her of Victor Drake.

"I want you to do a rather unpleasant job for me, Ruth."

She looked at him inquiringly. No need to say that certainly she would do it. That was understood.

"Every family's got a black sheep," said George.

She nodded comprehendingly.

"This is a cousin of my wife's—a thorough bad hat, I'm afraid. He's half ruined his mother—a fatuous, sentimental soul who has sold out most of what few shares she has on his behalf. He started by forging a check at Oxford—they got that hushed up and since then he's been shipped about the world—never making good anywhere."

Ruth listened without much interest. She was familiar with the type. They grew oranges, started chicken farms, went as jackaroos to Australian stations, got jobs with meat freezing concerns in New Zealand. They never made good, never stayed anywhere long, and invariably got through any money that they had invested on their behalf. They had never interested her much. She preferred success.

"He's turned up now in London and I find he's been worrying my wife. She hadn't set eyes on him since she was a school-girl, but he's a plausible sort of scoundrel and he's been writing to her for money, and I'm not going to stand for that. I've made an appointment with him for twelve o'clock this morning at his hotel. I want you to deal with it for me. The fact is I don't want to get into contact with the fellow. I've never met him and I never want to and I don't want Rosemary to meet him. I think the whole thing can be kept absolutely business-like if it's fixed up through a third party."

"Yes, that is always a good plan. What is the arrangement to be?"

"A hundred pounds cash and a ticket to Rio de Janeiro. The money to be given him actually on board the boat."

Ruth smiled.

"Quite so. You want to be sure he actually sails!"

"I see you understand."

"It's not an uncommon case," she said indifferently.

28

"No, plenty of that type about." He hesitated. "Are you sure you don't mind doing this?"

"Of course not." She was a little amused. "I can assure you I am quite capable of dealing with the matter."

"You're capable of anything."

"What about booking his passage? What's his name, by the way?"

"Victor Drake. The ticket's here. I rang up the steamship company yesterday. It's the *San Cristobal,* sails from Tilbury tomorrow."

Ruth took the ticket, glanced over it to make sure of its correctness and put it into her handbag.

"That's settled. I'll see to it. Twelve o'clock. What address?"

"The Rupert, off Russell Square."

She made a note of it.

"Ruth, my dear, I don't know what I should do without you—" He put a hand on her shoulder affectionately; it was the first time he had ever done such a thing. "You're my right hand, my other self."

She flushed, pleased.

"I've never been able to say much—I've taken all you do for granted—but it's not really like that. You don't know how much I rely on you for everything—" he repeated, *"everything.* You're the kindest, dearest, most helpful girl in the world!"

Ruth said, laughing to hide her pleasure and embarrassment, "You'll spoil me saying such nice things."

"Oh, but I mean them. You're part of the firm, Ruth. Life without you would be unthinkable."

She went out feeling a warm glow at his words. It was still with her when she arrived at the Rupert Hotel on her errand.

Ruth felt no embarrassment at what lay before her. She was quite confident of her powers to deal with any situation. Hard luck stories and people never appealed to her. She was prepared to take Victor Drake as all in the day's work.

He was very much as she had pictured him, though perhaps definitely more attractive. She made no mistake in her estimate of his character. There was not much good

29

in Victor Drake. As cold-hearted and calculating a personality as could exist, well masked behind an agreeable deviltry. What she had not allowed for was his power of reading other people's souls, and the practised ease with which he could play on the emotions. Perhaps, too, she had overestimated her own resistance to his charm. For he had charm.

He greeted her with an air of delighted surprise.

"George's emissary? But how wonderful. What a surprise!"

In dry, even tones, she set out George's terms. Victor agreed to them in the most amiable manner.

"A hundred pounds? Not bad at all. Poor old George. I'd have taken sixty—but don't tell him so! Conditions: 'Do not worry lovely Cousin Rosemary—do not contaminate innocent Cousin Iris—do not embarrass worthy Cousin George.' All agreed to! Who is coming to see me off on the *San Cristobal*? You are, my dear Miss Lessing? Delightful." He wrinkled up his nose, his dark eyes twinkled sympathetically. He had a lean brown face and there was a suggestion about him of a Toreador—romantic conception! He was attractive to women and knew it!

"You've been with Barton some time, haven't you, Miss Lessing?"

"Six years."

"And he wouldn't know what to do without you! Oh, yes, I know all about it. And I know all about you, Miss Lessing."

"How do you know?" asked Ruth sharply.

Victor grinned.

"Rosemary told me."

"Rosemary? But—"

"That's all right. I don't propose to worry Rosemary any further. She's already been very nice to me—quite sympathetic. I got a hundred out of her, as a matter of fact."

"You—"

Ruth stopped and Victor laughed. His laugh was infectious. She found herself laughing, too.

"That's too bad of you, Mr. Drake."

"I'm a very accomplished sponger. Highly finished

technique. The mater, for instance, will always come across if I send a wire hinting at imminent suicide."

"You ought to be ashamed of yourself."

"I disapprove of myself very deeply. I'm a bad lot, Miss Lessing. I'd like *you* to know just how bad."

"Why?" She was curious.

"I don't know. You're different. I couldn't play up the usual technique to you. Those clear eyes of yours—you wouldn't fall for it. No, 'more sinned against than sinning, poor fellow' wouldn't cut any ice with you. You've no pity in you."

Her faced hardened.

"I despise pity."

"In spite of your name? Ruth *is* your name, isn't it? Piquant that. Ruth the ruthless."

She said, "I've no sympathy with weakness!"

"Who said I was weak? No, no, you're wrong there, my dear. Wicked, perhaps. But there's one thing to be said for me."

Her lip curled a little. The inevitable excuse.

"Yes?"

"I enjoy myself. Yes," he nodded, "I enjoy myself a good deal. I've seen a good deal of life, Ruth. I've done almost everything. I've been an actor and a storekeeper and a waiter and an odd job man, and a luggage porter, and a property man in a circus! I've sailed before the mast in a tramp steamer. I've been in the running for President in a South American Republic. I've been in prison! There are only two things I've never done, an honest day's work, or paid my own way."

He looked at her laughing. She ought, she felt, to have been revolted. But the strength of Victor Drake was the strength of the devil. He could make evil seem amusing. He was looking at her now with that uncanny penetration.

"You needn't look so smug, Ruth! You haven't as many morals as you think you have! Success is your fetish. You're the kind of girl who ends up by marrying the boss. That's what you ought to have done with George. George oughtn't to have married that little ass Rosemary.

He ought to have married *you*. He'd have done a damned sight better for himself if he had."

"I think you're rather insulting."

"Rosemary's a damned fool, always has been. Lovely as paradise and dumb as a rabbit. She's the kind men fall for but never stick to. Now you—you're different. My God, if a man fell in love with you—he'd never tire."

He had reached the vulnerable spot. She said with sudden raw sincerity, "If! But he wouldn't fall in love with me!"

"You mean George didn't? Don't fool yourself, Ruth. If anything happened to Rosemary, George would marry you like a shot."

(Yes, that was it. That was the beginning of it all.)

Victor said, watching her, "But you know that as well as I do."

(George's hand on hers, his voice affectionate, warm —Yes, surely it was true . . . He turned to her, depended on her . . .)

Victor said gently, "You ought to have more confidence in yourself, my dear girl. You could twist George around your little finger. Rosemary's only a silly little fool."

"It's true," Ruth thought. "If it weren't for Rosemary, I could make George ask me to marry him. I'd be good to him. I'd look after him well."

She felt a sudden blind anger, an uprushing of passionate resentment. Victor Drake was watching her with a good deal of amusement. He liked putting ideas into people's heads. Or, as in this case, showing them the ideas that were already there.

Yes, that was how it started—that chance meeting with a man who was going to the other side of the globe on the following day. The Ruth who came back to the office was not quite the same Ruth who had left it, though no one could have noticed anything different in her manner or appearance.

Shortly after she had returned to the office Rosemary Barton rang up on the telephone.

"Mr. Barton has just gone out to lunch. Can I do anything?"

"Oh, Ruth, would you? That tiresome Colonel Race

has sent a telegram to say he won't be back in time for my party. Ask George who he'd like to ask instead. We really ought to have another man. There are four women —Iris is coming as a treat and Sandra Farraday and— who on earth's the other? I can't remember."

"I'm the fourth, I think. You very kindly asked me."

"Oh, of course, I'd forgotten all about you!"

Rosemary's laugh came light and tinkling. She could not see the sudden flush, the hard line of Ruth Lessing's jaw.

Asked to Rosemary's party as a favour—a concession to George! "Oh, yes, we'll have your Ruth Lessing. After all she'll be pleased to be asked, and she is awfully useful. She looks quite presentable, too."

In that moment Ruth Lessing knew that she hated Rosemary Barton.

Hated her for being rich and beautiful and careless and brainless. No routine hard work in an office for Rosemary—everything handed to her on a golden platter. Love affairs, a doting husband—no need to work or plan—

Hateful, condescending, stuck-up frivolous beauty. . . .

"I wish you were dead," said Ruth Lessing in a low voice to the silent telephone.

Her own words startled her. They were so unlike her. She had never been passionate, never vehement, never been anything but cool and controlled and efficient.

She said to herself, "What's happening to me?"

She had hated Rosemary Barton that afternoon. She still hated Rosemary Barton on this day a year later.

Some day, perhaps, she would be able to forget Rosemary Barton. But not yet.

She deliberately sent her mind back to those November days.

Sitting looking at the telephone—feeling hatred surge up in her heart. . . .

Giving Rosemary's message to George in her pleasant controlled voice. Suggesting that she herself should not come so as to leave the number even. George had quickly overridden *that!*

Coming in to report next morning on the sailing of the *San Cristobal.* George's relief and gratitude.

33

"So he's sailed on her all right?"

"Yes. I handed him the money just before the gangway was taken up." She hesitated and said, "He waved his hand as the boat backed away from the quay and called out, 'Love and kisses to George and tell him I'll drink his health tonight.'"

"Impudence!" said George. He asked curiously, "What did you think of him, Ruth?"

Her voice was deliberately colourless as she replied, "Oh—much as I expected. A weak type."

And George saw nothing, noticed nothing! She felt like crying out, "Why did you send me to see him? Didn't you know what he might do to me? Don't you realize that I'm a different person since yesterday? Can't you see that I'm dangerous? That there's no knowing what I may do?"

Instead she said in her businesslike voice, "About that São Paulo letter—"

She was the competent efficient secretary . . .

Five more days.

Rosemary's birthday.

A quiet day at the office—a visit to the hair-dresser—the putting on of a new black frock, a touch of make-up skilfully applied. A face looking in the glass that was not quite her own face. A pale, determined, bitter face.

It was true what Victor Drake had said. There was no pity in her.

Later, when she was staring across the table at Rosemary Barton's blue convulsed face, she still felt no pity.

Now, eleven months later, thinking of Rosemary Barton, she felt suddenly afraid . . .

CHAPTER 3   ANTHONY BROWNE

ANTHONY BROWNE was frowning into the middle distance as he thought about Rosemary Barton.

A damned fool he had been ever to get mixed up with her. Though a man might be excused for that! Certainly she was easy upon the eyes. That evening at the Dorchester he'd been able to look at nothing else. As beautiful as a houri—and probably just about as intelligent!

Still he'd fallen for her rather badly. Used up a lot of energy trying to find someone who would introduce him. Quite unforgiveable really when he ought to have been attending strictly to business. After all, he wasn't idling his days away at Claridge's for pleasure.

But Rosemary Barton was lovely enough in all conscience to excuse any momentary lapse from duty. All very well to kid himself now and wonder why he'd been such a fool. Fortunately there was nothing to regret. Almost as soon as he spoke to her the charm had faded a little. Things resumed their normal proportions. This wasn't love—nor yet infatuation. A good time was to be had by all, no more, no less.

Well, he'd enjoyed it. And Rosemary had enjoyed it, too. She danced like an angel and wherever he took her men turned round to stare at her. It gave a fellow a pleasant feeling. So long as you didn't expect her to talk. He thanked his stars he wasn't married to her. Once you got used to all that perfection of face and form, where would you be? She couldn't even listen intelligently. The sort of girl who would expect you to tell her every morning at the breakfast table that you loved her passionately!

Oh, all very well to think those things now.

He'd fallen for her all right, hadn't he?

Danced attendance on her. Rung her up, taken her out, danced with her, kissed her in the taxi. Been in a fair way to make rather a fool of himself over her until that startling, that incredible day.

He could remember just how she had looked, the piece of chestnut hair that had fallen loose over one ear, the lowered lashes, and the gleam of her dark blue eyes through them. The pout of the soft red lips.

"Anthony Browne. It's a nice name!"

He said lightly: "Eminently well established and respectable. There was a chamberlain to Henry VIII called Anthony Browne."

"An ancestor, I suppose?"

"I wouldn't swear to that."

"You'd better not!"

He raised his eyebrows.

"I'm the Colonial branch."

"Not the Italian one?"

"Oh," he laughed. "My olive complexion? I had a Spanish mother."

"That explains it."

"Explains what?"

"A great deal, Mr. Anthony Browne."

"You're very fond of my name."

"I said so. It's a nice name."

And then quickly, like a bolt from the blue: "Nicer than Tony Morelli."

For a moment he could hardly believe his ears! It was incredible! Impossible!

He caught her by the arm. In the harshness of his grip she winced away.

"Oo, you're hurting me!"

"Where did you get hold of that name?"

His voice was harsh, menacing.

She laughed, delighted with the effect she had produced. The incredible little fool!

"Who told you?"

"Someone who recognized you."

"Who was it? This is serious, Rosemary. I've got to know."

She shot a sideways glance at him.

"A disreputable cousin of mine, Victor Drake."

"I've never met anyone of that name."

"I imagine he wasn't using that name at the time you knew him. Saving the family feelings."

Anthony said slowly, "I see. It was—in prison?"

"Yes. I was reading Victor the riot act—telling him he was a disgrace to us all. He didn't care, of course. Then he grinned and said, 'You aren't always so particular yourself, sweetheart. I saw you the other night dancing with an ex-jailbird—one of your best boy friends, in fact. Calls himself Anthony Browne, I heard, but in stir he was Tony Morelli.' "

Anthony said in a light voice, "I must renew my acquaintance with this friend of my youth. We old prison ties must stick together."

Rosemary shook her head.

"Too late. He's been shipped off to South America. He sailed yesterday."

"I see." Anthony drew a deep breath. "So you're the only person who knows my guilty secret?"

She nodded. "I won't tell on you."

"You'd better not." His voice grew stern. "Look here, Rosemary, this is dangerous. You don't want your lovely face carved up, do you? There are people who don't stick at a little thing like ruining a girl's beauty. And there's such a thing as being bumped off. It doesn't only happen in books and films. It happens in real life, too."

"Are you threatening me, Tony?"

"Warning you."

Would she take the warning? Did she realize that he was in deadly earnest? Silly little fool. No sense in that lovely empty head. You couldn't rely on her to keep her mouth shut. All the same he'd have to try and ram his meaning home.

"Forget you ever heard the name of Tony Morelli, do you understand?"

"But I don't mind a bit, Tony. I'm quite broad-minded. It's quite a thrill for me to meet a criminal. You needn't feel ashamed of it."

The absurd little idiot. He looked at her coldly. He wondered in that moment how he could have ever fancied he cared. He'd never been able to suffer fools gladly—not even fools with pretty faces.

"Forget about Tony Morelli," he said grimly. "I mean it. Never mention that name again."

He'd have to get out. That was the only thing to do. There was no relying on this girl's silence. She'd talk whenever she felt inclined.

She was smiling at him—an enchanting smile, but it left him unmoved.

"Don't be so fierce. Take me to the Jarrows' dance next week."

"I shan't be here. I'm going away."

"Not before my brithday party. You can't let me down.

I'm counting on you. Now don't say no. I've been miserably ill with that horrid 'flu' and I'm still feeling terribly weak. I mustn't be crossed. You've got to come."

He might have stood firm. He might have chucked it all—gone right away.

Instead, through an open door, he saw Iris coming down the stairs, Iris, very straight and slim, with her pale face and black hair and grey eyes. Iris with much less than Rosemary's beauty and with all the character that Rosemary would never have.

In that moment he hated himself for having fallen a victim, in however small a degree, to Rosemary's facile charm. He felt as Romeo felt remembering Rosalind when he had first seen Juliet.

Anthony Browne changed his mind.

In the flash of a second he committed himself to a totally different course of action.

CHAPTER 4   STEPHEN FARRADAY

STEPHEN FARRADAY was thinking of Rosemary—thinking of her with that incredulous amazement that her image always aroused in him. Usually he banished all thoughts of her from his mind as promptly as they arose—but there were times when, persistent in death as she had been in life, she refused to be thus arbitrarily dismissed.

His first reaction was always the same, a quick, irresponsible shudder as he remembered the scene in the restaurant. At least he need not think again of *that*. His thoughts turned further back, to Rosemary alive, Rosemary smiling, breathing, gazing into his eyes . . .

What a fool—what an incredible fool he had been!

And amazement held him, sheer bewildered amazement. How had it all come about? He simply could not understand it. It was as though his life were divided into two parts, one, the larger part, a sane, well-balanced, orderly progression, the other a brief, uncharacteristic madness. The two parts simply did not fit.

For with all his ability and his clever, shrewd intellect, Stephen had not the inner perception to see that actually they fitted only too well.

Sometimes he looked back over his life, appraising it coldly and without undue emotion, but with a certain priggish self-congratulation. From a very early age he had been determined to succeed in life, and in spite of difficulties and certain initial disadvantages he *had* succeeded.

He had always had a certain simplicity of belief and outlook. He believed in the Will. What a man willed, that he could do!

Little Stephen Farraday had steadfastly cultivated his Will. He could look for little help in life save that which he got by his own efforts. A small pale boy of seven, with a good forehead and a determined chin, he meant to rise—and rise high. His parents, he already knew, would be of no use to him. His mother had married beneath her station in life—and regretted it. His father, a small builder, shrewd, cunning and cheeseparing, was despised by his wife and also by his son . . . For this mother, vague, aimless, and given to extraordinary variations of mood, Stephen felt only a puzzled incomprehension until the day when he found her slumped down on the corner of a table with an empty eau de cologne bottle fallen from her hand. He had never thought of drink as an explanation of his mother's moods. She never drank spirits or beer, and he had never realized that her passion for eau de cologne had had any other origin than her vague explanation of headaches.

He realized in that moment that he had little affection for his parents. He suspected shrewdly that they had not much for him. He was small for his age, quiet, with a tendency to stammer. Namby-pamby his father called him. A well-behaved child, little trouble in the house. His father would have preferred a more rumbustious type. "Always getting into mischief *I* was, at his age." Sometimes, looking at Stephen, he felt uneasily his own social inferiority to his wife. Stephen took after her folk.

Quietly, with growing determination, Stephen mapped out his own life. He was going to succeed. As a first test of will, he determined to master his stammer. He practised speaking slowly, with a slight hesitation between every word. And in time his efforts were crowned with success. He no longer stammered. In school he applied himself to his lessons. He intended to have education. Education got you somewhere. Soon his teachers became interested, encouraged him. He won a scholarship. His parents were approached by the educational authorities—the boy had promise. Mr. Farraday, doing well out of a row of jerry-built houses, was persuaded to invest money in his son's education.

At twenty-two, Stephen came down from Oxford with a good degree, a reputation as a good and witty speaker, and a knack of writing articles. He had also made some useful friends. Politics were what attracted him. He had learned to overcome his natural shyness and to cultivate an admirable social manner—modest, friendly, and with that touch of brilliance that led people to say, "That young man will go far." Though by predilection a Liberal, Stephen realized that for the moment, at least, the Liberal Party was dead. He joined the ranks of the Labour Party. His name soon became known as that of a "coming" young man. But the Labour Party did not satisfy Stephen. He found it less open to new ideas, more hidebound by tradition than its great and powerful rival. The Conservatives, on the other hand, were on the lookout for a promising young talent.

They approved of Stephen Farraday—he was just the type they wanted. He contested a fairly solid Labour constituency and won it by a very narrow majority. It was with a feeling of triumph that Stephen took his seat in the House of Commons. His career had begun and this was the right career he had chosen. Into this he could put all his ability, all his ambition. He felt in him the ability to govern, and to govern well. He had a talent for handling people, for knowing when to flatter and when to oppose. One day—he swore it—he would be in the Cabinet.

Nevertheless, once the excitement of being actually in

the House had subsided, he experienced swift disillusion-
ment. The hardly fought election had put him in the limelight, now he was down in the rut, a mere insignificant
unit of the rank and file, subservient to the party whips,
and kept in his place. It was not easy here to rise out of
obscurity. Youth here was looked upon with suspicion.
One needed something above ability. One needed influence.

There were certain interests. Certain families. You had
to be sponsored.

He considered marriage. Up to now he had thought
very little about the subject. He had had a dim picture in
the back of his mind of some handsome creature who
would stand hand in hand with him sharing his life and
his ambitions; who would give him children and to whom
he could unburden his thoughts and perplexities. Some
woman who felt as he did and who would be eager for
his success and proud of him when he achieved it.

Then one day he went to one of the big receptions at
Kidderminster House. The Kidderminster connection was
the most powerful in England. They were, and had always been, a great political family. Lord Kidderminster,
with his little imperial, his tall distinguished figure, was
known by sight everywhere. Lady Kidderminster's large
rocking-horse face was familiar on public platforms and
on committees all over England. They had five daughters,
three of them beautiful, but all serious-minded, and one
son still at Eton.

The Kidderminsters made a point of encouraging likely
young members of the Party. Hence Farraday's invitation.

He did not know many people there and he was standing alone near a window about twenty minutes after his
arrival. The crowd by the tea table was thinning out and
passing into the other rooms when Stephen noticed a tall
girl in black standing alone by the table looking for a
moment slightly at a loss.

Stephen Farraday had a very good eye for faces. He
had picked up that very morning in the Tube a *Home
Gossip* discarded by a woman traveller and had glanced
over it with slight amusement. There had been a rather

smudgy reproduction of Lady Alexandra Hayle, third daughter of the Earl of Kidderminster, and below it a gossipy little extract about her: "—always been of a shy and retiring disposition—devoted to animals—Lady Alexandra has taken a course in Domestic Science, as Lady Kidderminster believes in her daughters being thoroughly grounded in all domestic subjects."

That was Lady Alexandra Hayle standing there, and with the unerring perception of a shy person, Stephen knew that she, too, was shy. The plainest of the five daughters, Alexandra had always suffered under a sense of inferiority. Given the same education and upbringing as her sisters, she had never quite attained their *savoir-faire*, which annoyed her mother considerably. Sandra must make an effort—it was absurd to appear so awkward, so gauche.

Stephen did not know that, but he knew that the girl was ill at ease and unhappy. And suddenly a rush of conviction came to him. This was his chance! *Take it, you fool, take it! It's now or never!*

He crossed the room to the long buffet. Standing beside the girl, he picked up a sandwich. Then, turning, and speaking nervously and with an effort (no acting, that—he *was* nervous!), he said, "I say, do you mind if I speak to you? I don't know many people here and I can see you don't either. Don't snub me. As a matter of fact I'm awfully s-s-shy" (his stammer of years ago came back at a most opportune moment; "and—and I think you're s-s-shy too, aren't you—"

The girl flushed—her mouth opened. But, as he had guessed, she could not say it. Too difficult to find words to say, "I'm the daughter of the house." Instead she admitted quietly, "As a matter of fact, I—I am shy. I always have been."

Stephen went on quickly, "It's a horrible feeling. I don't know whether one ever gets over it. Sometimes I feel absolutely tongue-tied."

"So do I."

He went on—talking rather quickly, stammering a little —his manner was boyish, appealing. It was a manner that had been natural to him a few years ago and which was now consciously retained and cultivated. It was young, naïve, disarming.

He led the conversation soon to the subject of plays, mentioned one that was running which had attracted a good deal of interest. Sandra had seen it. They discussed it. It had dealt with some point of the social services and they were soon deep in a discussion of these measures.

Stephen did not overdo things. He saw Lady Kidderminster entering the room, her eyes in search of her daughter. It was no part of his plan to be introduced now. He murmured a good-bye.

"I have enjoyed talking to you. I was simply hating the whole show till I found you. Thank you."

He left Kidderminster House with a feeling of exhilaration. He had taken his chance. Now to consolidate what he had started.

For several days after that he haunted the neighbourhood of Kidderminster House. Once Sandra came out with one of her sisters. Once she left the house alone, but with a hurried step. He shook his head. That would not do; she was obviously en route to some particular appointment. Then, about a week after the party, his patience was rewarded. She came out one morning with a small black Scotty dog and she turned with a leisurely step in the direction of the park.

Five minutes later a young man, walking rapidly in the opposite direction, pulled up short and stopped in front of Sandra. He exclaimed blithely, "I say, what luck! I wondered if I'd ever see you again."

His tone was so delighted that she blushed just a little.

He stooped to the dog.

"What a jolly little fellow. What's his name?"

"MacTavish."

"Oh, very Scotch."

They talked dog for some moments. Then Stephen said, with a trace of embarrassment, "I never told you my name the other day. It's Farraday. Stephen Farraday. I'm an obscure M.P."

He looked at her inquiringly and saw the colour come up in her cheeks again as she said, "I'm Alexandra Hayle."

He responded to that very well. He might have been back in the O.U.D.S. Surprise, recognition, dismay, embarrassment!

"Oh, you're—you're Lady Alexandra Hayle—you—my goodness! *What* a stupid fool you must have thought me the other day!"

Her answering move was inevitable. She was bound both by her breeding and her natural kindliness to do all she could to put him at his ease, to reassure him.

"I ought to have told you at the time."

"I ought to have known. What an oaf you must think me!"

"How should you have known? What does it matter anyway? Please, Mr. Farraday, don't look so upset. Let's walk to the Serpentine. Look, MacTavish is simply pulling."

After that, he met her several times in the park. He told her his ambitions. Together they discussed political topics. He found her intelligent, well-informed and sympathetic. She had good brains and a singularly unbiased mind. They were friends now.

The next advance came when he was asked to dinner at Kidderminster House and to go on to a dance. A man had fallen through at the last moment. When Lady Kidderminster was racking her brains Sandra said quietly, "What about Stephen Farraday?"

"Stephen Farraday?"

"Yes, he was at your party the other day and I've met him once or twice since."

Lord Kidderminster was consulted and was all in favour of encouraging the young hopefuls of the political world.

"Brilliant young fellow—quite brilliant. Never heard of his people but he'll make a name for himself one of these days."

Stephen came and acquitted himself well.

"A useful young man to know," said Lady Kidderminster with unconscious arrogance.

Two months later Stephen put his fortunes to the test. They were by the Serpentine and MacTavish sat with his head on Stephen's foot.

"Sandra, do you know—you must know that I love you. I want you to marry me. I wouldn't ask you if I didn't believe that I shall make a name for myself one day. I do believe it. You shan't be ashamed of your choice. I swear it."

She said, "I'm not ashamed."

"Then do you care?"

"Didn't you know?"

"I hoped—but I couldn't be sure. Do you know that I've loved you since that very first moment when I saw you across the room and took my courage in both hands and came to speak to you. I was never more terrified in my life."

She said, "I think I loved you then, too . . ."

It was not all plain sailing. Sandra's quiet announcement that she was going to marry Stephen Farraday sent her family into immediate protests. Who was he? What did they know about him?

To Lord Kidderminster, Stephen was quite frank about his family and origin. He spared a fleeting thought that it was just as well for his prospects that his parents were now both dead.

To his wife, Lord Kidderminster said, "H'm, it might be worse."

He knew his daughter fairly well, knew that her quiet manner hid inflexible purpose. If she meant to have the fellow she would have him. She'd never give in!

"The fellow's got a career ahead of him. With a bit of backing he'll go far. Heaven knows we could do with some young blood. He seems a decent chap, too."

Lady Kidderminster assented grudgingly. It was not at all her idea of a good match for her daughter. Still, Sandra was certainly the most difficult of the family. Susan had been a beauty and Esther had brains. Diana, clever child, had married the young Duke of Harwich—the *parti* of the season. Sandra had certainly less charm—there was her shyness—and if this young man had a future as everyone seemed to think . . .

She capitulated, murmuring, "But, of course, one will have to use *influence* . . ."

So Alexandra Catherine Hayle took Stephen Leonard

Farraday for better and for worse, in white satin and Brussels lace, with six bridesmaids and two minute pages and all the accessories of a fashionable wedding. They went to Italy for the honeymoon and came back to a small charming house in Westminster, and a short time afterwards Sandra's godmother died and left her a very delightful small Queen Anne manor house in the country. Everything went well for the young married pair. Stephen plunged into Parliamentary life with renewed ardour, Sandra aided and abetted him in every way, identifying herself heart and soul with his ambitions. Sometimes, Stephen would think with an almost incredulous realization of how Fortune had favoured him! His alliance with the powerful Kidderminster faction assured him of a rapid rise in his career. His own ability and brilliance would consolidate the position that opportunity made for him. He believed honestly in his own powers and was prepared to work unsparingly for the good of his country.

Often, looking across the table at his wife, he felt gladly what a perfect helpmate she was—just what he had always imagined. He liked the lovely clean lines of her head and neck, the direct hazel eyes under their level brows, the rather high white forehead and the faint arrogance of her aquiline nose. She looked, he thought, rather like a race-horse—so well-groomed, so instinct with breeding, so proud. He found her an ideal companion; their minds raced alike to the same quick conclusions. Yes, he thought, Stephen Farraday, that little disconsolate boy, had done very well for himself. His life was shaping exactly as he had meant it to be. He was only a year or two over thirty and already success lay in the hollow of his hand.

And in that mood of triumphant satisfaction, he went with his wife for a fortnight to St. Moritz and, looking across the hotel lounge, saw Rosemary Barton.

What happened to him at that moment he never understood. By a kind of poetic revenge the words he had once spoken to another woman came true. Across a room he fell in love. Deeply, overwhelmingly, crazily in love. It was the kind of desperate, headlong, adolescent calf love that he should have experienced years ago and got over.

He had always assumed that he was not a passionate type of man. One or two ephemeral affairs, a mild flirtation—that, so far as he knew, was all that "love" meant to him. Sensual pleasures simply did not appeal to him. He told himself that he was too fastidious for that sort of thing.

If he had been asked if he loved his wife, he would have replied "Certainly"—yet he knew, well enough, that he would not have dreamed of marrying her if she had been, say, the daughter of a penniless country gentleman. He liked her, admired her and felt a deep affection for her and also a very real gratitude for what her position had brought him.

That he could fall in love with the abandon and misery of a callow boy was a revelation. He could think of nothing but Rosemary. Her lovely laughing face, the rich chestnut of her hair, her swaying voluptuous figure. He couldn't eat—he couldn't sleep. They went skiing together. He danced with her. And as he held her to him he knew that he wanted her more than anything on earth. So this, this misery, this aching, longing agony—this was love!

Even in his preoccupation he blessed Fate for having given him a naturally imperturbable manner. No one must guess, no one must know, what he was feeling—except Rosemary herself.

The Bartons left a week earlier than the Farradays. Stephen said to Sandra that St. Moritz was not very amusing. Should they cut short their time and go back to London? She agreed very amiably. Two weeks after their return, he became Rosemary's lover.

A strange, ecstatic, hectic period—feverish, unreal. It lasted—how long? Six months at most. Six months during which Stephen went about his work as usual, visited his constituency, asked questions in the House, spoke at various meetings, discussed politics with Sandra and thought of one thing only—Rosemary.

Their secret meetings in the little flat, her beauty, the passionate endearments he showered on her, her clinging, passionate embraces. A dream. A sensual, infatuated dream.

And after the dream—the awakening.

It seemed to happen quite suddenly.

Like coming out of a tunnel into the daylight.

One day he was a bemused lover, the next day he was Stephen Farraday again, thinking that, perhaps, he ought not to see Rosemary quite so often. Dash it all, they had been taking some terrific risks. If Sandra were ever to suspect— he stole a look at her face down the breakfast table. Thank goodness, she didn't suspect. She hadn't an idea. Yet some of his excuses for absence lately had been pretty thin. Some women would have begun to smell a rat. Thank goodness, Sandra wasn't a suspicious woman.

He took a deep breath. Really, he and Rosemary had been very unwise! It was a wonder her husband hadn't got wise to things. One of these foolish, unsuspecting chaps—years older than she was.

What a lovely creature she was . . .

He thought suddenly of golf links. Fresh air blowing over sand dunes, tramping round with clubs—swinging a driver—a nice clean shot off the tee—a little chip with a mashie. Men. Men in plus fours smoking pipes. And no women allowed on the links!

He said suddenly to Sandra, "Couldn't we go down to Fairhaven?"

She looked up, surprised.

"Do you want to? Can you get away?"

"Might take the inside of a week. I'd like to get some golf. I feel stale."

"We could go tomorrow if you like. It will mean putting off the Astleys, and I must cancel that meeting on Tuesday. But what about the Lovats?"

"Oh, let's cancel that, too. We can think of some excuse. I want to get away."

It had been peaceful at Fairhaven with Sandra and the dogs on the terrace and in the old walled garden, and with golf at Sandley Heath, and pottering down to the farm in the evening with MacTavish at his heels.

He had felt rather like someone who is recovering from an illness.

He had frowned when he saw Rosemary's writing. He'd told her not to write. It was too dangerous. Not that Sandra ever asked him who his letters were from, but all the same it was unwise. Servants weren't always to be trusted.

He ripped open the envelope with some annoyance, having taken the letter into his study. Pages. Simply pages.

As he read, the old enchantment swept over him again. She adored him, she loved him more than ever, she couldn't endure not seeing him for five whole days. Was he feeling the same? Did the Leopard miss his Ethiopian?

He half-smiled, half-sighed. That ridiculous joke—born when he had bought her a man's spotted dressing-gown that she had admired. The Leopard changing his spots and he had said, "But you mustn't change your skin, darling." And after that she had called him Leopard and he called her his Black Beauty.

Damned silly, really. Yes, damned silly. Rather sweet of her to have written such pages and pages. But still she shouldn't have done it. Dash it all, they'd got to be *careful!* Sandra wasn't the sort of woman who would stand for anything of that kind. If she once got an inkling— Writing letters was dangerous. He'd told Rosemary so. Why couldn't she wait until he got back to town? Dash it all, he'd see her in another two or three days.

There was another letter on the breakfast table the following morning. This time Stephen swore inwardly. He thought Sandra's eyes rested on it for a couple of seconds. But she didn't say anything. Thank goodness she wasn't the sort of woman who asked questions about a man's correspondence.

After breakfast he took the car over to the market town eight miles away. Wouldn't do to put through a call from the village. He got Rosemary on the phone.

"Hullo—that you, Rosemary? Don't write any more letters."

"Stephen, darling, how lovely to hear your voice!"

"Be careful; can anyone overhear you?"

"Of course not. Oh, angel, I have missed you. Have you missed me?"

"Yes, of course. But don't write. It's much too risky."

"Did you like my letter? Did it make you feel I was with you? Darling, I want to be with you every minute. Do you feel that too?"

"Yes—but not on the phone, old thing."

"You're so ridiculously cautious. What does it matter?"

"I'm thinking of you, too, Rosemary. I couldn't bear any trouble to come to you through me."

"I don't care what happens to me. You know that."

"Well, I care, sweetheart."

"When are you coming back?"

"Tuesday."

"And we'll meet at the flat Wednesday."

"Yes—er, yes."

"Darling, I can hardly bear to wait. Can't you make some excuse and come up today? Oh, Stephen, you *could!* Politics or something stupid like that?"

"I'm afraid it's out of the question."

"I don't believe you miss me half as much as I miss you."

"Nonsense, of course I do."

When he rang off he felt tired. Why should women insist on being so damned reckless? Rosemary and he must be more careful in the future. They'd have to meet less often.

Things after that became difficult. He was busy—very busy. It was quite impossible to give as much time to Rosemary—and the trying thing was she didn't seem able to understand. He explained but she just wouldn't listen.

"Oh, your stupid old politics—as though *they* were important."

"But they *are*—"

She didn't realize. She didn't care. She took no interest in his work, in his ambitions, in his career. All she wanted was to hear him reiterate again and again that he loved her. "Just as much as ever? Tell me again that you *really* love me?"

Surely, he thought, she might take that for granted by this time! She was a lovely creature, lovely—but the trouble was that you couldn't *talk* to her.

The trouble was they'd been seeing too much of each

other. You couldn't keep up an affair at fever heat. They must meet less often—slacken off a bit.

But that made her resentful—very resentful. She was always reproaching him now.

"You don't love me as you used to do."

And then he'd have to reassure her, to swear that of course he did. And she *would* constantly resurrect everything he had ever said to her.

"Do you remember when you said it would be lovely if we died together? Fell asleep for ever in each other's arms? Do you remember when you said we'd take a caravan and go off into the desert? Just the stars and the camels—and how we'd forget everything in the world?"

What damned silly things one said when one was in love! They hadn't seemed fatuous at the time, but to have them hashed up in cold blood! Why couldn't women let things decently alone? A man didn't want to be continually reminded what an ass he'd made of himself.

She came out with sudden unreasonable demands. Couldn't he go abroad to the South of France and she'd meet him there? Or go to Sicily or Corsica—one of those places where you never saw anyone you knew? Stephen said grimly that there was no such place in the world. At the most unlikely spots you always met some dear old school friend that you'd never seen for years.

And then she said something that frightened him.

"Well, but it wouldn't really matter, would it?"

He was alert, watchful, suddenly cold within.

"What do you mean?"

She was smiling up at him, that same enchanting smile that had once made his heart turn over and his bones ache with longing. Now it made him merely impatient.

"Leopard, darling, I've thought sometimes that we're stupid to go on trying to carry on this hole and corner business. Let's stop pretending. George will divorce me and your wife will divorce you and then we can get married."

Just like that! Disaster! Ruin! And she couldn't see it!

"I wouldn't let you do such a thing."

"But, darling, I don't care. I'm not really very conventional."

"But I am. But I am," thought Stephen.

"I do feel that love is the most important thing in the world. It doesn't matter what people think of us."

"It would matter to me, my dear. An open scandal of that kind would be the end of my career." .

"But would that really matter? There are hundreds of other things that you could do."

"Don't be silly."

"Why have you got to do anything anyway? I've got lots of money you know. Of my own, I mean, not George's. We could wander about all over the world, going to the most enchanting out of the way places—places, perhaps, where nobody else has ever been. Or to some island in the Pacific—think of it, the hot sun and the blue sea and coral reefs."

He did think of it. A South Sea Island! Of all the idiotic ideas. What sort of man did she think he was—a beach-comber?

He looked at her with eyes from which the last traces of scales had fallen. A lovely creature with the brains of a hen! He'd been mad—utterly and completely mad. But he was sane again now. And he'd got to get out of this fix. Unless he was careful she'd ruin his whole life.

He said all the things that hundreds of men had said before him. They must end it all—so he wrote. It was only fair to her. He couldn't risk bringing unhappiness on her. She didn't understand—and so on and so on.

It was all over—he must make her understand that.

But that was just what she refused to understand. It wasn't to be as easy as that. She adored him, she loved him more than ever, she couldn't live without him! The only honest thing was for her to tell her husband, and for Stephen to tell his wife the *truth!* He remembered how cold he had felt as he sat holding her letter. The little fool! The silly clinging fool! She'd go and blab the whole thing to George Barton and then George Barton would divorce her and cite him as co-respondent. And Sandra would perforce divorce him, too. He hadn't any doubt of that. She had spoken once of a friend, had said with faint surprise, "But, of course, when she found out he was having an affair with another woman, what else could she do but divorce him?" That was what Sandra would feel. She was proud. She would never share a man.

And then he would be done, finished—the influential Kidderminster backing would be withdrawn. It would be the kind of scandal that he would not be able to live down, even though public opinion was broader-minded than it used to be. But not in a flagrant case like this! Good-bye to his dreams, his ambitions. Everything wrecked, broken—all because of a crazy infatuation for a silly woman. Calf love, that was all it had been. Calf love contracted at the wrong time of life.

He'd lose everything he'd staked. Failure! Ignominy!

He'd lose Sandra . . .

And suddenly, with a shock of surprise, he realized that it was that he would mind most. *He'd lose Sandra.* Sandra with her square white forehead and her clear hazel eyes. Sandra, his dear friend and companion, his arrogant proud loyal Sandra. No, he couldn't lose Sandra—he couldn't . . . Anything but that.

The perspiration broke out on his forehead.

Somehow he *must* get out of this mess.

Somehow he must make Rosemary listen to reason . . . But would she? Rosemary and reason didn't go together. Supposing he were to tell her that, after all, he loved his wife? No. She simply wouldn't believe it. She was such a stupid woman. Empty-headed, clinging, possessive. And she loved him still—that was the mischief of it.

A kind of blind rage rose up in him. How on earth was he to keep her quiet? To shut her mouth? Nothing short of a dose of poison would do that, he thought bitterly.

A wasp was buzzing close at hand. He stared abstractedly. It had got inside a cut glass jampot and was trying to get out.

Like me, he thought, entrapped by sweetness and now —he can't get out, poor devil.

But he, Stephen Farraday, was going to get out somehow. Time, he must play for time.

Rosemary was down with "flu" at the moment. He'd sent conventional inquiries—a big sheaf of flowers. It gave him a respite. Next week Sandra and he were dining with the Bartons—a birthday party for Rosemary. Rosemary had said, "I shan't do anything until after my birthday—it would be too cruel to George. He's making such a fuss about it. He's such a dear. After it's all over we'll come to an understanding."

Supposing he were to tell her brutally that it was all over, that he no longer cared? He shivered. No, he dare not do that. She might go to George in hysterics. She might even come to Sandra. He could hear her tearful, bewildered voice.

"He says he doesn't care any more, but I *know* it's not true. He's trying to be loyal—to play the game with *you*—but I know you'll agree with me that when people love each other honesty is the *only* way. That's why I'm asking you to give him his freedom."

That was just the sort of nauseating stuff she would pour out. And Sandra, her face proud and disdainful, would say, "He can have his freedom!"

She wouldn't believe—how could she believe? But if Rosemary were to bring out those letters—the letters he'd been asinine enough to write to her. Heaven knew what he had said in them. Enough and more than enough to convince Sandra—letters such as he had never written to *her*—

He must think of something—some way of keeping Rosemary quiet.

"It's a pity," he thought grimly, "that we don't live in the days of the Borgias . . ."

A glass of poisoned champagne was about the only thing that would keep Rosemary quiet.

Yes, he had actually thought that.

Cyanide of potassium in her champagne glass, cyanide of potassium in her evening bag. Depression after influenza.

And across the table, Sandra's eyes meeting his.

Nearly a year ago—and he couldn't forget.

CHAPTER 5   ALEXANDRA FARRADAY

SANDRA FARRADAY had not forgotten Rosemary Barton.

She was thinking of her at this very minute—thinking of her slumped forward across the table in the restaurant that night.

She remembered her own sharp indrawn breath and how then, looking up, she had found Stephen watching her . . .

Had he read the truth in her eyes? Had he seen the hate and the mingling of horror and triumph?

Nearly a year ago now—and as fresh in her mind as if it had been yesterday! Rosemary, that's for remembrance. How horribly true that was. It was no good a person being dead if they lived on in your mind. That was what Rosemary had done. In Sandra's mind—and in Stephen's, too? She didn't know, but she thought it probable.

The Luxembourg—that hateful place with its excellent food, its deft swift service, its luxurious *décor* and setting. An impossible place to avoid, people were always asking you there.

She would have liked to forget—but everything conspired to make her remember. Even Fairhaven was no longer exempt now that George Barton had come to live at Little Priors.

It was really rather extraordinary of him. George Barton was altogether an odd man. Not at all the kind of neighbour she liked to have. His presence at Little Priors spoiled for her the charm and peace of Fairhaven. Always, up to this summer, it had been a place of healing and rest, a place where she and Stephen had been happy—that is, if they ever had been happy.

Her lips pressed thinly together. Yes, a thousand times, yes! They could have been happy but for Rosemary. It was Rosemary who had shattered the delicate edifice of mutual trust and tenderness that she and Stephen were beginning to build.

Something, some instinct, had bade her hide from Stephen her own passion, her single-hearted devotion. She had loved him from the moment he came across the room to her that day at Kidderminster House, pretending to be shy, pretending not to know who she was.

For he *had* known. She could not say when she had first accepted that fact. Some time after their marriage, one day when he was expounding some neat piece of political manipulation necessary to the passing of some Bill.

The thought had flashed across her mind then, "This reminds me of something. What?" Later she realized that it was, in essence, the same tactics he had used that day at Kidderminster House. She accepted the knowledge without surprise, as though it were something of which she had long been aware, but which had only just risen to the surface of her mind.

From the day of their marriage she had realized that he did not love her in the same way as she loved him. But she thought it possible that he was actually incapable of such a love. That power of loving was her own unhappy heritage. To care with a desperation, an intensity that was, she knew, unusual among women! She would have died for him willingly; she was ready to lie for him, scheme for him, suffer for him! Instead she accepted with pride and reserve the place he wanted her to fill. He wanted her co-operation, her sympathy, her active and intellectual help. He wanted of her, not her heart, but her brains, and those material advantages which birth had given her.

One thing she would never do, embarrass him by the expression of a devotion to which he could make no adequate return. And she did believe honestly that he liked her, that he took pleasure in her company. She foresaw a future in which her burden would be immeasurably lightened—a future of tenderness and friendship.

In this way, she thought, he loved her. . . .

And then Rosemary came.

She wondered sometimes, with a wry, painful twist of

the lips, how it was that he could imagine that she did not know. She had known from the first minute—up there at St. Moritz—when she had first seen the way he looked at the woman.

She had known the very day the woman became his mistress.

She knew the scent the creature used. . . .

She could read in Stephen's polite face, with eyes abstracted, just what his memories were, what he was thinking about—that woman—the woman he had just left!

It was difficult, she thought dispassionately, to assess the suffering she had been through. Enduring, day after day, the tortures of the damned, with nothing to carry her through but her belief in courage—her own natural pride. She would not show, she would never show, what she was feeling. She lost weight, grew thinner and paler, the bones of her head and shoulders showing more distinctly with the flesh stretched tightly over them. She forced herself to eat, but could not force herself to sleep. She lay long nights, with dry eyes, staring into darkness. She despised the taking of drugs as weakness. She would hang on. To show herself hurt, to plead, to protest—all those things were abhorrent to her.

She had one crumb of comfort, a meagre one—Stephen did not wish to leave her. Granted that that was for the sake of his career, not out of fondness for her, still the fact remained. He did not want to leave her.

Some day, perhaps, the infatuation would pass. . . .

What could he, after all, see in the girl? She was attractive, beautiful—but so were other women. What did he find in Rosemary Barton that infatuated him?

She was brainless, silly, and not—she clung to this point especially—not even particularly amusing. If she had had wit—charm and provocation of manner—those were the things that held men. Sandra clung to the belief that the thing would end—that Stephen would tire of it.

She was convinced that the main interest in his life was his work. He was marked out for great things and he knew it. He had a fine statesmanlike brain and he delighted in using it. It was his appointed task in life. Surely

57

once the infatuation began to wane he would realize that fact?

Never for one minute did Sandra consider leaving him. The idea never even came to her. She was his body and soul, to take or discard. He was her life, her existence. Love burned in her with a medieval force.

There was a moment when she had hope. They went down to Fairhaven. Stephen seemed more his normal self. She felt suddenly a renewal of the old sympathy between them. Hope rose in her heart. He wanted her still, he enjoyed her company, he relied on her judgment. For the moment, he had escaped from the clutches of that woman.

He looked happier, more like his own self.

Nothing was irretrievably ruined. He was getting over it. If only he could make up his mind to break with her. . . .

Then they went back to London and Stephen relapsed. He looked haggard, worried, ill. He began to be unable to fix his mind on his work.

She thought she knew the cause. Rosemary wanted him to go away with her. He was making up his mind to take the step—to break with everything he cared about most. Folly! Madness! He was the type of man with whom his work would always come first—a very English type. He must know that himself, deep down. Yes, but Rosemary was very lovely—and very stupid. Stephen would not be the first man who had thrown away his career for a woman and been sorry afterwards!

Sandra caught a few words—a phrase one day at a cocktail party.

"—telling George—got to make up our minds."

It was soon after that that Rosemary went down with "flu."

A little hope rose in Sandra's heart. Suppose she were to get pneumonia—people did after "flu"—a young friend of hers had died that way only last winter. If Rosemary were to die—

She did not try to repress the thought—she was not horrified at herself. She was medieval enough to hate with a steady and untroubled mind.

She hated Rosemary Barton. If thoughts could kill, she would have killed her.

But thoughts do not kill—

Thoughts are not enough.

How beautiful Rosemary had looked that night at the Luxembourg with her pale fox furs slipping off her shoulders in the ladies' cloakroom. Thinner, paler since her illness—an air of delicacy made her beauty more ethereal. She had stood in front of the glass touching up her face.

Sandra, behind her, looked at their joint reflection in the mirror. Her own face like something sculptured, cold, lifeless. No feeling there you would have said—a cold hard woman.

And then Rosemary said, "Oh, Sandra, am I taking all the glass? I've finished now. This horrid 'flu' has pulled me down a lot. I look a sight. And I feel quite weak still and headachy."

Sandra had asked with quiet polite concern, "Have you got a headache tonight?"

"Just a bit of one. You haven't got an aspirin, have you?"

"I've got a Cachet Faivre."

She had opened her handbag, taken out the cachet. Rosemary had accepted it. "I'll take it in my bag in case."

That competent, dark-haired girl, Barton's secretary, had watched the little transaction. She came in turn to the mirror, and just put on a light dusting of powder. A nice looking girl, almost handsome. Sandra had the impression that she didn't like Rosemary.

Then they had gone out of the cloakroom, Sandra first, then Rosemary, then Miss Lessing—oh, and, of course, the girl Iris, Rosemary's sister; she had been there. Very excited, with big grey eyes, and a schoolgirlish white dress.

They had gone out and joined the men in the hall.

And the head waiter had come bustling forward and showed them to their table. They had passed in under the great domed arch and there had been nothing, absolutely nothing, to warn one of them that she would never come out through that door again alive. . . .

ROSEMARY . . .

George Barton lowered his glass and stared rather owlishly into the fire.

He had drunk just enough to feel maudlin with self-pity.

What a lovely girl she had been. He'd always been crazy about her. She knew it, but he'd always supposed she'd only laugh at him.

Even when he first asked her to marry him, he hadn't done it with any conviction. Mowed and mumbled. Acted like a blithering fool.

"You know, old girl, any time—you've only got to say. I know it's no good. You wouldn't look at me. I've always been the most awful fool. Got a bit of a corporation, too. But you do know what I feel, don't you, eh? I mean—I'm always there. Know I haven't got an earthly chance, but thought I'd just mention it."

And Rosemary had laughed and kissed the top of his head.

"You're sweet, George, and I'll remember the kind offer, but I'm not marrying anyone just at present."

And he had said seriously, "Quite right. Take plenty of time to look around. You can take your pick."

He'd never had any hope—not any real hope.

That's why he had been so incredulous, so dazed when Rosemary had said she was going to marry him.

She wasn't in love with him, of course. He knew that quite well. In fact, she admitted as much.

"You do understand, don't you? I want to feel settled down and happy and safe. I shall with you. I'm so sick of being in love. It always goes wrong somehow and ends in a mess. I like you, George. You're nice and funny and sweet and you think I'm wonderful. That's what I want."

He had answered rather incoherently, "Steady does it. We'll be as happy as kings."

Well, that hadn't been far wrong. They had been happy. He'd always felt humble in his own mind. He'd always told himself that there were bound to be snags. Rosemary wasn't going to be satisfied with a dull kind of chap like himself. There would be *incidents!* He'd schooled himself to accept—incidents! He would hold firm to the belief that they wouldn't be lasting; Rosemary would always come back to him. Once let him accept that view and all would be well.

For she was fond of him. Her affection for him was constant and unvarying. It existed quite apart from her flirtations and her love affairs.

He had schooled himself to accept those. He had told himself that they were inevitable with someone of Rosemary's susceptible temperament and unusual beauty. What he had not bargained for were his own reactions.

Flirtations with this young man and that were nothing, but when he first got an inkling of a serious affair—

He'd known quick enough, sensed the difference in her. The rising excitement, the added beauty, the whole glowing radiance. And then what his instinct told him was confirmed by ugly concrete fact.

There was that day when he'd come into her sitting room and she had instinctively covered with her hand the page of the letter she was writing. He'd known then. She was writing to her lover.

Presently, when she went out of the room, he went across to the blotter. She had taken the letter with her, but the blotting sheet was nearly fresh. He'd taken it across the room and held it up to the glass—had seen the words in Rosemary's dashing script, "My own beloved darling. . . ."

His blood had sung in his ears. He understood in that moment just what Othello had felt. Wise resolutions? Pah! Only the natural man counted. He'd like to choke the life out of her! He'd like to murder the fellow in cold blood. Who was it? That fellow Browne? Or that stick Stephen Farraday? They'd both of them been making sheep's-eyes at her.

He caught sight of his face in the glass. His eyes were suffused with blood. He looked as though he were going to have a fit.

As he remembered that moment, George Barton let his glass fall from his hand. Once again he felt the choking sensation, the beating blood in his ears. Even now—

With an effort he pushed remembrance away. Mustn't go over that again. It was past—done with. He wouldn't ever suffer like that again.

Rosemary was dead. Dead and at peace. And he was at peace too. No more suffering.

Funny to think that that was what her death had meant to him.

Peace. . . .

He'd never even told Ruth that. Good girl, Ruth. A good headpiece on her. Really, he didn't know what he would do without her. The way she helped. The way she sympathized. And never a hint of sex. Not man mad like Rosemary . . .

Rosemary. Rosemary sitting at the round table in the restaurant. A little thin in the face after "flu"—a little pulled down—but lovely, so lovely. And only an hour later—

No, he wouldn't think of that. Not just now. His plan. He would think of The Plan.

He'd speak to Race first. He'd show Race the letters. What would Race make of those letters? Iris had been dumbfounded. She evidently hadn't had the slightest idea.

Well, he was in charge of the situation now. He'd got it all taped.

The Plan. All worked out. The date. The place.

November first. All Saints' Day. That was a good touch. The Luxembourg, of course. He'd try to get the same table.

And the same guests Anthony Browne, Stephen Farraday, Sandra Farraday. Then, of course, Ruth and Iris and himself. And as the odd seventh guest, he'd get Race. Race who was originally to have been at the dinner.

And there would be one empty place.

It would be splendid!

Dramatic!

A repetition of the crime.
Well, not quite a repetition. . . .
His mind went back.
Rosemary's birthday. . . .
Rosemary, sprawled forward on that table—dead. . . .

BOOK II

ALL SAINTS' DAY

"There's Rosemary, that's for remembrance."

CHAPTER I

LUCILLA DRAKE was twittering. That was the term always used in the family and it was really a, very apt description of the sounds that issued from Lucilla's kindly lips.

She was concerned on this particularly morning with many things—so many that she found it hard to pin her attention down to one at a time. There was the imminence of the move back to town and the household problems involved in that move. Servants, housekeeping, winter storage, a thousand minor details—all these contended with a concern over Iris's looks.

"Really, dear, I feel quite anxious about you—you look so white and washed out—as though you hadn't slept—did you sleep? If not, there's that nice sleeping preparation of Dr. Wylie's—or was it Dr. Gaskell's?—which reminds me—I shall have to go and speak to the grocer *myself*—either the maids have been ordering in things on their own, or else it's deliberate swindling on his part. Packets and packets of soap flakes—and I never allow more than three a week. But perhaps a tonic would be better? Easton's syrup, they used to give when I was a girl. And spinach, of course. I'll tell cook to have spinach for lunch today."

Iris was too languid and too used to Mrs. Drake's discursive style to inquire why the mention of Dr. Gaskell should have reminded her aunt of the local grocer, though had she done so, she would have received the immediate response, "Because the grocer's name is Cranford, my dear." Aunt Lucilla's reasoning was always crystal clear to herself.

Iris merely said with what energy she could command, "I'm perfectly well, Aunt Lucilla."

"Black under the eyes," said Mrs. Drake. "You've been doing too much."

"I've done nothing at all for weeks."

"So you think, dear. But too much tennis is overtiring for young girls. And I think the air down here is inclined to be enervating. This place is in a hollow. If George had consulted *me* instead of that girl."

"Girl?"

"That Miss Lessing he thinks so much of. All very well in the office, I dare say—but a great mistake to take her out of her place. Encourage her to think herself one of the family. Not that she needs much encouragement, I should say."

"Oh, well, Aunt Lucilla, Ruth *is* practically one of the family."

Mrs. Drake sniffed.

"She means to be—that's quite clear. Poor George— really an infant in arms where women are concerned. But it won't do, Iris. George must be protected from himself and if I were you I should make it very clear that nice as Miss Lessing is, any idea of marriage is out of the question."

Iris was startled for a moment out of her apathy.

"I never thought of George marrying Ruth."

"You don't see what goes on under your nose, child. Of course, you haven't had my experience of life." Iris smiled in spite of herself. Aunt Lucilla was really very funny sometimes. "That young woman is out for matrimony."

"Would it matter?" asked Iris.

"Matter? Of course it would matter."

"Wouldn't it really be rather nice?" Her aunt stared at

her. "Nice for George, I mean. I think you're right about her, you know. I think she is fond of him. And she'd be an awfully good wife to him and look after him."

Mrs. Drake snorted and an almost indignant expression appeared on her rather sheep-like, amiable face.

"George is very well looked after at present. What more can he want, I should like to know? Excellent meals and his mending seen to. Very pleasant for him to have an attractive young girl like you about the house and when you marry some day, I should hope I was still capable of seeing to his comfort and looking after his health. Just as well or better than a young woman out of an office could do—what else does she know about housekeeping? Figures and ledgers and shorthand and typing—what good is that in a man's home?"

Iris smiled and shook her head, but she did not argue the point. She was thinking of the smooth dark satin of Ruth's head, of the clear complexion and the figure so well set off by the severe tailor-mades that Ruth affected. Poor Aunt Lucilla, all her mind on comfort and housekeeping, with romance so very far behind her that she had probably forgotten what it meant—if indeed, thought Iris, remembering her uncle by marriage, it had ever meant much.

Lucilla Drake had been Hector Marle's half-sister, the child of an earlier marriage. She had played the little mother to a very much younger brother when his own mother died. Housekeeping for her father, she had stiffened into a pronounced spinsterhood. She was close on forty when she met the Rev. Caleb Drake, he himself a man of over fifty. Her married life had been short, a mere two years, then she had been left a widow with an infant son. Motherhood, coming late and unexpectedly, had been the supreme experience of Lucilla Drake's life. Her son had turned out an anxiety, a source of grief and a constant financial drain—but never a disappointment. Mrs. Drake refused to recognize anything in her son Victor except an amiable weakness of character. Victor was too trusting—too easily led astray by bad companions because of his own belief in them. Victor was unlucky. Victor was deceived. Victor was swindled. He was the cat's-paw of wicked men who exploited his innocence. The pleasant, rather silly sheep's face hardened into obstinacy when criticism of Victor was to the fore. She knew her own son. He was a dear boy, full of high spirits, and his so-called friends took advantage of him. She knew, none better, how Victor hated having to ask her for money. But when the poor boy was really in such a terrible situation, what else could he do? It wasn't as though he had anyone but her to go to.

All the same, as she admitted, George's invitation to come and live in the house and look after Iris had come as a godsend, at a moment when she really had been in desperate straits of genteel povery. She had been very happy and comfortable this last year and it was not in human nature to look kindly on the possibility of being superseded by an upstart young woman, all modern efficiency and capability, who in any case, so she persuaded herself, would only be marrying George for his money. Of course that was what she was after! A good home and a rich, indulgent husband. You couldn't tell Aunt Lucilla, at her age, that any young woman really *liked* working for her living! Girls were the same as they always had been—if they could get a man to keep them in comfort, they much preferred it. This Ruth Lessing was clever, worming her way into a position of confidence, advising George about house furnishing, making herself indispensable—but thank goodness, there was *one* person at least who saw what she was up to!

Lucilla Drake nodded her head several times, causing her soft double chins to quiver, raised her eyebrows with an air of superb human sapience, and abandoned the subject for one equally interesting and possibly even more pressing.

"It's the blankets I can't make up my mind about, dear. You see, I can't get it clearly laid down whether we shan't be coming down again until next spring or whether George means to run down for week-ends. He won't say."

"I suppose he doesn't really know." Iris tried to give her attention to a point that seemed completely unimportant. "If it was nice weather it might be fun to come down occasionally. Though I don't think I want to particularly. Still the house will be here if we do want to come."

"Yes, dear, but one wants to *know*. Because, you see, if we aren't coming down until next year, then the blankets ought to be put away with moth balls. But if we *are* coming down, that wouldn't be necessary, because the blankets would be *used*—and the smell of moth balls is so unpleasant."

"Well, don't use them."

"Yes, but it's been such a hot summer there are a lot of moths about. Everyone says it's a bad year for moths. And for wasps, of course. Hawkins told me yesterday he's taken thirty wasps' nests this summer—thirty—just fancy—"

Iris thought of Hawkins—stalking out at dusk—cyanide in hand—*cyanide—Rosemary*—why did everything lead back to that?

The thin trickle of sound that was Aunt Lucilla's voice was going on—it had reached by now a different point—

"—and whether one ought to send the silver to the bank or not? Lady Alexandra was saying so many burglaries—though of course we do have good shutters— I don't like the way she does her hair myself—it makes her face look so hard—but I should think she was a hard woman. And nervy, too. Everyone is nervy nowadays. When I was a girl people didn't know what nerves were. Which reminds me that I don't like the look of George lately—I wonder if he could be going to have 'flu'? I've wondered once or twice whether he was feverish. But perhaps it is some business worry. He looks to me, you know, as though he has got something on his mind."

Iris shivered, and Lucilla Drake exclaimed triumphantly, "There, I said you had a chill."

CHAPTER 2

"How I wish they had never come here."

Sandra Farraday uttered the words with such unusual bitterness that her husband turned to look at her in surprise. It was as though his own thoughts had been put into words—the thoughts that he had been trying so hard to conceal. So Sandra, too, felt as he did? She, too, had felt that Fairhaven was spoiled, its peace impaired, by these new neighbours a mile away across the park.

He said, voicing his surprise impulsively, "I didn't know you felt like that about them, too."

Immediately, or so it seemed to him, she withdrew into herself.

"Neighbours are so important in the country. One has either to be rude or friendly; one can't, as in London, just keep people as amiable acquaintances."

"No," said Stephen, "one can't do that."

"And now we're committed to this extraordinary party."

They were both silent, running over in their minds the scene at lunch. George Barton had been friendly, even exuberant in manner, with a kind of undercurrent of excitement of which they had both been conscious. George Barton was really very odd these days. Stephen had never noticed him much in the time preceding Rosemary's death. George had just been there in the background, the kindly, dull husband of a young and beautiful wife. Stephen had never even felt a pang of disquiet over the betrayal of George. George had been the kind of husband who was born to be betrayed. So much older—so devoid of the attractions necessary to hold an attractive and capricious woman. Had George himself been deceived? Stephen did not think so. George, he thought, knew Rosemary very well. He loved her, and he was the kind of man who was humble about his own powers of holding a wife's interest.

All the same, George must have suffered.

Stephen began to wonder just what George had felt when Rosemary died.

He and Sandra had seen little of him in the months following the tragedy. It was not until he had suddenly appeared as near neighbour at Little Priors that he had re-entered their lives and at once, so Stephen thought, he had seemed different.

More alive, more positive. And—yes, decidedly *odd*.

He had been odd today. That suddenly blurted-out invitation. A party for Iris's eighteenth birthday. He did so hope Stephen and Sandra would both come. Stephen and Sandra had been so kind to them down here.

Sandra had said quickly, of course, it would be delightful. Naturally Stephen would be rather tied up when they got back to London and she herself had a great many tiresome engagements, but she did hope they would be able to manage it.

"Then let's settle a day now, shall we?"

George's face—florid, smiling, insistent.

"I thought perhaps one day the week after next—Wednesday or Thursday? Thursday is November first. Would that be all right? But we'll arrange any day that suits you both."

It had been the kind of invitation that pinned you down—there was a certain lack of social *savoir-faire*. Stephen noticed that Iris Marle had gone red and looked embarrassed. Sandra had been perfect. She had smilingly surrendered to the inevitable and said that Thursday, November first, would suit them very well.

Suddenly voicing his thoughts, Stephen said sharply, "We needn't go."

Sandra turned her face slightly towards him. It wore a thoughtful considering air.

"You think not?"

"It's easy to make some excuse."

"He'll only insist on us coming some other time—or change the day. He—he seems very set on our coming."

"I can't think why. It's Iris's party—and I can't believe she is so particularly anxious for our company."

"No—no—" She sounded thoughtful.

Then she said, "You know where this party is to be?"

"No."

"The Luxembourg."

The shock nearly deprived him of speech. He felt the colour ebbing out of his cheeks. He pulled himself together and met her eyes. Was it his fancy or was there meaning in the level gaze?

"But it's preposterous," he exclaimed, blustering a little in his attempt to conceal his own personal emotion. "The Luxembourg where—to revive all that. The man must be mad."

"I thought of that," said Sandra.

"But then we shall certainly refuse to go. The—the whole thing was terribly unpleasant. You remember all the publicity—the pictures in the papers."

"I remember the unpleasantness," said Sandra.

"Doesn't he realize how disagreeable it would be for us?"

"He has a reason, you know, Stephen. A reason that he gave me."

"What was it?"

He felt thankful that she was looking away from him when she spoke.

"He took me aside after lunch. He said he wanted to explain. He told me that the girl—Iris—had never recovered properly from the shock of her sister's death."

She paused and Stephen said unwillingly, "Well, I dare say that may be true enough—she looks far from well. I thought at lunch how ill she was looking."

"Yes, I noticed it, too—although she has seemed in good health and spirits on the whole lately. But I am telling you what George Barton said. He told me that Iris has consistently avoided the Luxembourg ever since, as far as she was able."

"I don't wonder."

"But according to him that is all wrong. It seems he consulted a nerve specialist on the subject—one of these modern men—and his advice is that after a shock of any kind, the trouble must be faced, not avoided. The principle, I gather, is like that of sending up an airman again immediately after a crash."

"Does the specialist suggest another suicide?"

Sandra replied quietly, "He suggests that the associations of the restaurant must be overcome. It is, after all, just a restaurant. He proposed an ordinary pleasant party with, as far as possible, the same people present."

"Delightful for the people!"

"Do you mind so much, Stephen?"

A swift pang of alarm shot through him. He said quickly, "Of course I don't mind. I just thought it rather a gruesome idea. Personally *I* shouldn't mind in the least. . . . I was really thinking of *you*. If you don't mind—"

She interrupted him.

"I do mind. Very much. But the way George Barton put it made it very difficult to refuse. After all, I have frequently been to the Luxembourg since—so have you. One is constantly being asked there."

"But not under these circumstances."

"No."

Stephen said, "As you say, it is difficult to refuse— and if we put it off the invitation will be renewed. But there's no reason, Sandra, why *you* should have to endure it. I'll go and you can cry off at the last minute—a headache, chill—something of that kind."

He saw her chin go up.

"That would be cowardly. No, Stephen, if you go, I go. After all"—she laid her hand on his arm—"however little our marriage means, it should at least mean sharing our difficulties."

But he was staring at her—rendered dumb by one poignant phrase which had escaped her so easily, as though it voiced a long familiar and not very important fact.

Recovering himself he said, "Why do you say that? *However little our marriage means?*"

She looked at him steadily. "Isn't it true?"

"No, a thousand times no. Our marriage means everything to me."

She smiled.

"I suppose it does—in a way. We're a good team, Stephen. We pull together with a satisfactory result."

72

"I didn't mean that." He found his breath was coming unevenly. He took her hand in both of his, holding it very closely. "Sandra, don't you know that you mean all the world to me?"

And suddenly she did know it. It was incredible—unforeseen, but it was so.

She was in his arms and he was holding her close, kissing her, stammering out incoherent words.

"Sandra—Sandra—darling. I love you . . . I've been so afraid—so afraid I'd lose you."

She heard herself saying, "Because of Rosemary?"

"Yes." He let go of her, stepped back; his face was ludicrous in its dismay.

"You knew—about Rosemary?"

"Of course—all the time."

"And you understood?"

She shook her head.

"No, I don't understand. I don't think I ever shall. You loved her?"

"Not really. It was you I loved."

A surge of bitterness swept over her. She quoted: "From the first moment you saw me across the room? Don't repeat that lie—for it was a lie!"

He was not taken aback by that sudden attack. He seemed to consider her words thoughtfully.

"Yes, it was a lie—and yet in a queer way it wasn't. I'm beginning to believe that it was true. Oh, try and *understand*, Sandra. You know the people who always have a noble and good reason to mask their meaner actions? The people who 'have to be honest' when they want to be unkind, who 'thought it their duty to repeat so and so,' who are such hypocrites to themselves that they go through to their life's end convinced that every mean and beastly action was done in a spirit of unselfishness! Try and realize that the opposite of those people can exist, too. People who are so cynical, so distrustful of themselves and of life that they can only believe in their bad motives. You were the woman I needed. That, at least, is true. And I do honestly believe, now, looking back on it, that if it hadn't been true, I should never have gone through with it."

She said, bitterly, "You were not in love with me."

"No, I'd never been in love. I was a starved, sexless creature who prided himself—yes, I did—on the fastidious coldness of his nature! And then I did fall in love 'across a room'—a silly, violent, puppy love. A thing like a mid-summer thunderstorm, brief, unreal, quickly over." He added bitterly, "Indeed a 'tale told by an idiot, full of sound and fury, signifying nothing'!"

He paused, and then went on, "It was here, at Fairhaven, that I woke up and realized the truth."

"The truth?"

"That the only thing in life that mattered to me was you—and keeping your love."

She murmured, "If I had only known."

"What did you think?"

"I thought you were planning to go away with her."

"With Rosemary?" He gave a short laugh. "That would indeed have been penal servitude for life!"

"Didn't she want you to go away with her?"

"Yes, she did."

"What happened?"

Stephen drew a deep breath. They were back again. Facing once more than intangible menace. He said, "The Luxembourg happened."

They were both silent, seeing, they both knew, the same thing. The blue, cyanosed face of a once lovely woman.

Staring at a dead woman, and then—looking up to meet each other's eyes . . .

Stephen said, "Forget it, Sandra, for God's sake, let us forget it!"

"It's no use forgetting. We're not going to be allowed to forget."

There was a pause. Then Sandra said, "What are we going to do?"

"What you said just now. Face things—together. Go to this horrible party whatever the reason for it may be."

"You don't believe what George Barton said about Iris."

"No. Do you?"

"It could be true. But even if it is, it's not the real reason."

"What do you think the real reason is?"

"I don't know, Stephen. But I'm afraid."

"Of George Barton?"

"Yes, I think he—knows."

Stephen said sharply, "Knows what?"

She turned her head slowly until her eyes met his.

She said in a whisper, "We mustn't be afraid. We must have courage—all the courage in the world. You're going to be a great man, Stephen—a man the world needs—and nothing shall interfere with that. I'm your wife and I love you."

"What do you think this party is, Sandra?"

"I think it's a trap."

He said slowly, "And we walk into it?"

"We can't afford to show we know it's a trap."

"No, that's true."

Suddenly Sandra threw back her head and laughed. She said, "Do your worst, Rosemary. You won't win."

Stephen gripped her shoulder.

"Be quiet, Sandra. Rosemary's dead."

"Is she? Sometimes—she seems very much alive. . . ."

CHAPTER 3

HALFWAY across the park Iris said, "Do you mind if I don't come back with you, George? I feel like a walk. I thought I'd go up over Friar's Hill and come down through the wood. I've had an awful headache all day."

"My poor child. Do go. I won't come with you—I'm expecting a fellow along some time this afternoon and I'm not quite sure when he'll turn up."

"Right. Good-bye till tea time."

She turned abruptly and made off at right angles to where a belt of larches showed on the hillside.

When she came out on the brow of the hill she drew a deep breath. It was one of those close humid days common in October. A dank moisture coated the leaves of the trees and the grey clouds hung low overhead promising yet more rain shortly. There was not really much more air up here on the hill than there had been in the valley, but, nevertheless, Iris felt as though she could breathe more freely.

She sat down on the trunk of a fallen tree and stared down into the valley to where Little Priors nestled demurely in its wooded hollow. Further to the left, Fairhaven Manor showed a gleam of white.

Iris stared out sombrely over the landscape, her chin cupped in her hand.

The slight rustle behind her was hardly louder than the drop of leaves, but she turned her head sharply as the branches parted and Anthony Browne came through them.

She cried half angrily, "Tony! Why do you always have to arrive like—like a demon in a pantomime?"

Anthony dropped to the ground beside her. He took out his cigarette case, offered her one and when she shook her head took one himself and lighted it. Then inhaling the first puff he replied, "It's because I'm what the papers call a Mystery Man. I *like* appearing from nowhere."

"How did you know where I was?"

"An excellent pair of bird glasses. I heard you were lunching with the Farradays and spied on you from the hillside when you left."

"Why don't you come to the house like an ordinary person?"

"I'm not an ordinary person," said Anthony in a shocked tone. "I'm very extraordinary."

"I think you are."

He looked at her quickly. Then he said, "Is anything the matter?"

"No, of course not. At least—"

She paused. Anthony said interrogatively, "At least?"

She drew a deep breath.

"I'm tired of being down here. I hate it. I want to go back to London."

"You're going soon, aren't you?"

"Next week."

"So this was a farewell party at the Farradays'?"

"It wasn't a party. Just them and one old cousin."

"Do you like the Farradays, Iris?"

"I don't know. I don't think I do very much—although I shouldn't say that because they've really been very nice to us."

"Do you think they like you?"

"No, I don't. I think they hate us."

"Interesting."

"Is it?"

"Oh, not the hatred—if true. I meant your use of the word 'us.' My question referred to you personally."

"Oh, I see . . . I think they like *me* quite well in a negative sort of way. I think it's us as a family living next door that they mind about. We weren't particular friends of theirs—they were Rosemary's friends."

"Yes," said Anthony, "as you say, they were Rosemary's friends—not that I should imagine Sandra Farraday and Rosemary were ever bosom friends, eh?"

"No," said Iris. She looked faintly apprehensive but Anthony smoked peacefully. Presently he said, "Do you know what strikes me most about the Farradays?"

"What?"

"Just that—that they are the Farradays. I always think of them like that—not as Stephen and Sandra, two individuals linked by the State and the Established Church—but as a definite dual entity—the Farradays. That is rarer than you would think. They are two people with a common aim, a common way of life, identical hopes and fears and beliefs. And the odd part of it is that they are actually very dissimilar in character. Stephen Farraday, I should say, is a man of very wide intellectual scope, extremely sensitive to outside opinion, horribly diffident about himself and somewhat lacking in moral courage. Sandra, on the other hand, has a narrow medieval mind, is capable of fanatical devotion, and is courageous to the point of recklessness."

"He always seems to me," said Iris, "rather pompous and stupid."

"He's not at all stupid. He's just one of the usual unhappy successes."

"Unhappy?"

"Most successes are unhappy. That's why they are successes—they have to reassure themselves about themselves by achieving something that the world will notice."

"What extraordinary ideas you have, Anthony."

"You'll find they're quite true if you only examine them. The happy people are failures because they are on such good terms with themselves that they don't give a damn. Like me. They are also usually agreeable to get on with—again like me."

"You have a very good opinion of yourself."

"I am just drawing attention to my good points in case you mayn't have noticed them."

Iris laughed. Her spirits had risen. The dull depression and fear had lifted from her mind. She glanced down at her watch.

"Come home and have tea, and give a few more people the benefit of your unusually agreeable society."

Anthony shook his head.

"Not today. I must be getting back."

Iris turned sharply on him.

"Why will you never come to the house? There must be a reason."

Anthony shrugged his shoulders.

"Put it that I'm rather peculiar in my ideas of accepting hospitality. Your brother-in-law doesn't like me—he's made that quite clear."

"Oh, don't bother about George. If Aunt Lucilla and I ask you—she's an old dear—you'd like her."

"I'm sure I should—but my objection holds."

"You use to come in Rosemary's time."

"That," said Anthony, "was rather different."

A faint cold hand touched Iris's heart. She said, "What made you come down here today? Had you business in this part of the world?"

"Very important business—with you. I came here to ask you a question, Iris."

The cold hand vanished. Instead there came a faint flutter, that throb of excitement that women have known from time immemorial. And with it Iris's face adopted that same look of blank inquiry that her great-grand-mother might have worn prior to saying a few minutes later, "Oh, Mr. X, this is so sudden!"

"Yes?" She turned that impossibly innocent face towards Anthony.

He was looking at her, his eyes were grave, almost stern.

"Answer me truthfully, Iris. This is my question. Do you trust me?"

It took her aback. It was not what she had expected. He saw that.

"You didn't think that that was what I was going to say? But it is a very important question, Iris. The most important question in the world to me. I ask it again. Do you trust me?"

She hesitated a bare second, then she answered, her eyes falling, "Yes."

"Then I'll go on and ask you something else. Will you come up to London and marry me without telling anybody about it?"

She stared.

"But I couldn't! I simply couldn't."

"You couldn't marry me?"

"Not in that way."

"And yet you love me. You do love me, don't you?"

She heard herself saying, "Yes, I love you, Anthony."

"But you won't come and marry me at the Church of Saint Elfrida, Bloomsbury, in the parish in which I have resided for some weeks and where I can consequently get married by license at any time?"

"How can I do a thing like that? George would be terribly hurt and Aunt Lucilla would never forgive me. And anyway, I'm not of age. I'm only eighteen."

"You'd have to lie about your age. I don't know what penalties I should incur for marrying a minor without her guardian's consent. Who is your guardian, by the way?"

"George. He's my trustee as well."

"As I was saying, whatever penalties I incurred, they couldn't unmarry us and that is really all I care about."

Iris shook her head. "I couldn't do it. I couldn't be so unkind. And in any case, *why?* What's the point of it?"

Anthony said, "That's why I asked you first if you

79

could trust me. You'd have to take my reasons on trust. Let's say that it is the simplest way. But never mind."

Iris said timidly, "If George only got to know you a little better. Come back now with me. It will be only he and Aunt Lucilla."

"Are you sure? I thought—" he paused. "As I struck up the hill I saw a man going up your drive—and the funny thing is that I believe I recognized him as a man I"—he hesitated—"had met."

"Of course—I forgot—George said he was expecting someone."

"The man I thought I saw was a man called Race—Colonel Race."

"Very likely," Iris agreed. "George does know a Colonel Race. He was coming to dinner on that night when Rosemary—"

She stopped, her voice quivering. Anthony gripped her hand.

"Don't go on remembering it, darling. It was beastly, I know."

She shook her head.

"I can't help it. Anthony—"

"Yes?"

"Did it ever occur to you—did you ever think—" She found a difficulty in putting her meaning into words.

"Did it ever strike you that—that Rosemary might not have committed suicide? That she might have been—*killed?*"

"Good God, Iris, what put that idea into your head?"

She did not reply—merely persisted, "That idea never occurred to you?"

"Certainly not. Of course Rosemary committed suicide."

Iris said nothing.

"Who's been suggesting these things to you?"

For a moment she was tempted to tell him George's incredible story, but she refrained. She said slowly, "It was just an idea."

"Forget it, darling idiot." He pulled her to her feet and kissed her cheek lightly. "Darling morbid idiot. Forget Rosemary. Only think of me."

CHAPTER 4

PUFFING at his pipe, Colonel Race looked speculatively at George Barton.

He had known George Barton ever since the latter's boyhood. Barton's uncle had been a country neighbour of the Races. There was a difference of nearly twenty years between the two men. Race was over sixty, a tall, erect, military figure, with sunburned face, closely cropped iron-grey hair, and shrewd dark eyes.

There had never been any particular intimacy between the two men—but Barton remained to Race "young George"—one of the many vague figures associated with earlier days.

He was thinking at this moment that he had really no idea what "young George" was like. On the brief occasions when they had met in later years, they had found little in common. Race was an out-of-door man, essentially of the empire builder type—most of his life had been spent abroad. George was emphatically the city gentleman. Their interests were dissimilar and when they met it was to exchange rather lukewarm reminiscences of "the old days," after which an embarrassed silence was apt to occur. Colonel Race was not good at small talk and might indeed have posed as the model of a strong silent man so beloved by an earlier generation of novelists.

Silent at this moment, he was wondering just why "young George" had been so insistent on this meeting. Thinking, too, that there was some subtle change in the man since he had last seen him a year ago. George Barton had always struck him as the essence of stodginess—cautious, practical, unimaginative.

There was, he thought, something very wrong with the fellow. Jumpy as a cat. He'd already re-lit his cigar three times—and that wasn't like Barton at all.

He took his pipe out of his mouth.

"Well, young George, what's the trouble?"

"You're right, Race, it is trouble. I want your advice badly—and your help."

The Colonel nodded and waited.

"Nearly a year ago you were coming to dine with us in London—at the Luxembourg. You had to go abroad at the last minute."

Again Race nodded.

"South Africa."

"At that dinner party my wife died."

Race stirred uncomfortably in his chair.

"I know. Read about it. Didn't mention it now or offer you sympathy because I didn't want to stir things up again. But I'm sorry, old man, you know that."

"Oh, yes, yes. That's not the point. My wife was supposed to have committed suicide."

Race fastened on the key word. His eyebrows rose.

"*Supposed?*"

"Read these."

He thrust the two letters into the other's hand. Race's eyebrows rose still higher.

"Anonymous letters?"

"Yes. And I believe them."

Race shook his head slowly.

"That's a dangerous thing to do. You'd be surprised how many lying, spiteful letters get written after any event that's been given any sort of publicity in the Press."

"I know that. But these weren't written at the time—they weren't written until six months afterwards."

Race nodded.

"That's a point. Who do you think wrote them?"

"I don't know. I don't care. The point is that I believe what they say is true. My wife was murdered."

Race laid down his pipe. He sat up a little straighter in his chair.

"Now just why do you think that? Had you any suspicion at the time? Had the police?"

"I was dazed when it happened—completely bowled over. I just accepted the verdict at the inquest. My wife had had the 'flu,' was run down. No suspicion of anything but suicide arose. The stuff was in her handbag, you see."

"What was the stuff?"

"Cyanide."

"I remember. She took it in champagne."

"Yes. It seemed, at the time, all quite straightforward."

"Had she ever threatened to commit suicide?"

"No, never. Rosemary," said George Barton, "loved life."

Race nodded. He had only met George's wife once. He had thought her a singularly lovely nit-wit—but certainly not a melancholic type.

"What about the medical evidence as to state of mind, et cetera?"

"Rosemary's own doctor—an elderly man who has attended the Marle family since they were children—was away on a sea voyage. His partner, a young man, attended Rosemary when she had 'flu.' All he said, I remember, was that the type of 'flu' about was inclined to leave very serious depression."

George paused and went on.

"It wasn't until after I got these letters that I talked with Rosemary's own doctor. I said nothing of the letters, of course—just discussed what had happened. He told me then that he was very surprised at what had happened. He would never have believed it, he said. Rosemary was not at all a suicidal type. It showed, he said, how even a patient one knew well might act in a thoroughly uncharacteristic manner."

Again George paused and then went on, "It was after talking to him that I realized how absolutely unconvincing to *me* Rosemary's suicide was. After all, I knew her very well. She was a person who was capable of violent fits of unhappiness. She could get very worked up over things, and she would on occasions take very rash and unconsidered action, but I have never known her in the frame of mind that 'wanted to get out of it all.' "

Race murmured in a slightly embarrassed manner, "Could she have had a motive for suicide apart from mere depression? Was she, I mean, definitely unhappy about anything?"

"I—no—she was perhaps rather nervy."

Avoiding looking at his friend, Race said, "Was she at

all a—melodramatic person? I only saw her once, you know. But there is a type that—well—might get a kick out of attempted suicide—usually if they've quarrelled with someone. The rather childish motive of 'I'll make them sorry!' "

"Rosemary and I hadn't quarrelled."

"No. And I must say that the fact of cyanide having been used rather rules that possibility out. It's not the kind of thing you can monkey about with safely—and everybody knows it."

"That's another point. If by any chance Rosemary *had* contemplated doing away with herself, surely she'd never do it that way? Painful and—and ugly. An overdose of some sleeping stuff would be far more likely."

"I agree. Was there any evidence as to her purchasing or getting hold of the cyanide?"

"No. But she had been staying with friends in the country and they had taken a wasps' nest one day. It was suggested that she might have taken a handful of potassium cyanide crystals then."

"Yes—it's not a difficult thing to get hold of. Most gardeners keep a stock of it."

He paused and then said, "Let me summarize the position. There was no positive evidence as to a disposition to suicide, or to any preparation for it. The whole thing was negative. But there can also have been no positive evidence pointing to murder, or the police would have got hold of it. They're quite awake, you know."

"The mere idea of murder would have seemed fantastic."

"But it didn't seem fantastic to you six months later?"

George said slowly, "I think I must have been unsatisfied all along. I think I must have been subconsciously preparing myself so that when I saw the thing written down in black and white I accepted it without any doubt."

"Yes." Race nodded. "Well, then, let's have it. Who do you suspect?"

George leaned forward—his face twitching.

"That's what is so terrible. *If* Rosemary was killed, one of those people round the table, one of our friends, must have done it. No one else came near the table."

"Waiters? Who poured out the wine?"

"Charles, the head waiter at the Luxembourg. You know Charles."

Race assented. Everybody knew Charles. It seemed quite impossible to imagine that Charles could have deliberately poisoned a client.

"And the waiter who looked after us was Giuseppe. We know Giuseppe well. I've known him for years. He always looks after me there. He's a delightful cheery little fellow."

"So we come down to the dinner party. Who was there?"

"Stephen Farraday, the M.P. His wife, Lady Alexandra Farraday. My secretary, Ruth Lessing. A fellow called Anthony Browne. Rosemary's sister Iris and myself. Seven in all. We should have been eight if you had come. When you dropped out, we couldn't think of anybody suitable to ask at the last minute."

"I see. Well, Barton, who do you think did it?"

George cried out, "I don't know—I tell you I don't know. If I had any idea—"

"All right—all right. I just thought you might have a definite suspicion. Well, it oughtn't to be difficult. How did you sit—starting with yourself?"

"I had Sandra Farraday on my right, of course. Next to her, Anthony Browne. Then Rosemary. Then Stephen Farraday, then Iris, then Ruth Lessing on my left."

"I see. And your wife had drunk champagne earlier in the evening?"

"Yes. The glasses had been filled up several times. It—it happened while the cabaret show was on. There was a lot of noise—it was one of those Negro shows and we were all watching it. She slumped forward on the table just before the lights went up. She may have cried out—or gasped—but nobody heard anything. The doctor said that death must have been practically instantaneous. Thank God for that."

"Yes, indeed. Well, Barton—on the face of it, it seems fairly obvious."

"You mean?"

"Stephen Farraday, of course. He was on her right

hand. Her champagne glass would be close to his left hand. Easiest thing in the world to put the stuff in as soon as the lights were lowered and general attention went to the raised stage. I can't see that anybody else had anything like as good an opportunity. I know those Luxembourg tables. There's plenty of room round, them—I doubt very much if anybody could have leaned across the table, for instance, without being noticed even if the lights were down. The same thing applies to the fellow on Rosemary's left. He would have had to lean across her to put anything in her glass. There *is* one other possibility, but we'll take the obvious person first. Any reason why Stephen Farraday, M.P., should want to do away with your wife?"

George said in a stifled voice, "They—they had been rather close friends. If—if Rosemary had turned him down, for instance, he might have wanted revenge."

"Sounds highly melodramatic. That is the only motive you can suggest?"

"Yes," said George. His face was very red. Race gave him the most fleeting of glances, then went on.

"We'll examine possibility Number Two. One of the women."

"Why the women?"

"My dear George, has it escaped your notice that in a party of seven, four women and three men, there will probably be one or two periods during the evening when three couples are dancing and one woman is sitting alone at the table? You did all dance?"

"Oh, yes."

"Good. Now before the cabaret, can you remember who was sitting alone at any moment?"

George thought a minute.

"I think—yes, Iris was odd man out last, and Ruth the time before."

"You don't remember when your wife drank champagne last?"

"Let me see, she had been dancing with Browne. I remember her coming back and saying that had been pretty strenuous—he's rather a fancy dancer. She drank up the wine in her glass then. A few minutes later they played

86

a waltz and she—she danced with me. She knew a waltz is the only dance I'm really any good at. Farraday danced with Ruth and Lady Alexandra with Browne. Iris sat out. Immediately after that, they had the cabaret."

"Then let's consider your wife's sister. Did she come into any money on your wife's death?"

George began to splutter.

"My dear Race—don't be absurd. Iris was a mere child, a schoolgirl."

"I've known two schoolgirls who committed murder."

"But Iris! She was devoted to Rosemary."

"Never mind, Barton. She had opportunity. I want to know if she had motive. Your wife, I believe, was a rich woman. Where did her money go—to you?"

"No, it went to Iris—a trust fund."

He explained the position, to which Race listened attentively.

"Rather a curious position. The rich sister and the poor sister. Some girls might have resented that."

"I'm sure Iris never did."

"Maybe not—but she had a motive all right. We'll try that tack now. Who else had a motive?"

"Nobody—nobody at all. Rosemary hadn't an enemy in the world, I'm sure. I've been looking into all that—asking questions—trying to find out. I've even taken this house near the Farradays so as to—"

He stopped. Race took up his pipe and began to scratch at its interior.

"Hadn't you better tell me everything, young George?"

"What do you mean?"

"You're keeping something back—it sticks out a mile. You can sit there defending your wife's reputation—or you can try and find out if she was murdered or not—but if the latter matters most to you, you'll have to come clean."

There was a silence.

"All right then," said George in a stifled voice. "You win."

"You'd reason to believe your wife had a lover; is that it?"

"Yes."

"Stephen Farraday?"

"I don't know! I swear to you I don't know! It might have been him or it might have been the other fellow, Browne. I couldn't make up my mind. It was hell."

"Tell me what you know about this Anthony Browne. Funny, I seem to have heard the name."

"I don't know anything about him. Nobody does. He's a good-looking amusing sort of chap—but nobody knows the first thing about him. He's supposed to be an American but he's got no accent to speak of."

"Oh, well, perhaps the Embassy will know something about him. You've no idea—which?"

"No—no, I haven't. I'll tell you, Race. She was writing a letter—I—I examined the blotting paper afterwards. It—it was a love letter all right—but there was no name."

Race turned his eyes away carefully.

"Well, that gives us a bit more to go on. Lady Alexandra, for instance—she comes into it, if her husband was having an affair with your wife. She's the kind of woman, you know, who feels things rather intensely. The quiet deep type. It's a type that will do murder at a pinch. We're getting on. There's Mystery Browne and Farraday and his wife, and young Iris Marle. What about this other woman, Ruth Lessing?"

"Ruth couldn't have had anything to do with it. She at least had no earthly motive."

"Your secretary, you say? What sort of a girl is she?"

"The dearest girl in the world." George spoke with enthusiasm. "She's practically one of the family. She's my right hand—I don't know anyone I think more highly of, or have more absolute faith in."

"You're fond of her," said Race, watching him thoughtfully.

"I'm devoted to her. That girl, Race, is an absolute trump. I depend on her in every way. She's the truest, dearest creature in the world."

Race murmured something that sounded like "Umhum" and left the subject. There was nothing in his manner to indicate to George that he had mentally chalked down a very definite motive to the unknown Ruth Lessing. He could imagine that this "dearest girl in the world" might have a very decided reason for wanting the removal of Mrs. George Barton to another world. It might be a mercenary motive—she might have envisaged herself as the second Mrs. Barton. It might be that she was genuinely in love with her employer. But the motive for Rosemary's death was there.

Instead he said gently, "I suppose it's occurred to you, George, that you had a pretty good motive yourself."

"I?" George looked flabbergasted.

"Well, remember Othello and Desdemona."

"I see what you mean. But—but it wasn't like that between me and Rosemary. I adored her, of course, but I always knew that there would be things that—that I'd have to endure. Not that she wasn't fond of me—she was. She was very fond of me and sweet to me always. But, of course, I'm a dull stick, no getting away from it. Not romantic, you know. Anyway, I'd made up my mind when I married her that it wasn't going to be all beer and skittles. She as good as warned me. It hurt, of course, when it happened—but to suggest that I'd have touched a hair of her head—"

He stopped, and then went on in a different tone, "Anyway, if I'd done it, why on earth should I go raking it all up? I mean, after a verdict of suicide, and everything all settled and over. It would be madness."

"Absolutely. That's why I don't seriously suspect you, my dear fellow. If you were a successful murderer and you got a couple of letters like these, you'd put them quietly in the fire and say nothing at all about it. And that brings me to what I think is the one really interesting feature of the whole thing. Who wrote those letters?"

"Eh?" George looked rather startled. "I haven't the least idea."

"The point doesn't seem to have interested you. It interests me. It's the first question I asked you. We can assume, I take it, that they weren't written by the murderer. Why should he queer his own pitch when, as you say, everything had settled down and suicide was universally accepted? Then who wrote them? Who is it who is interested in stirring the whole thing up again?"

"Servants?" hazarded George vaguely.

"Possibly. If so, what servants, and what do they know? Did Rosemary have a confidential maid?"

George shook his head.

"No. At the time we had a cook—Mrs. Pound—we've still got her, and a couple of maids. I think they've both left. They weren't with us very long."

"Well, Barton, if you want my advice, which I gather you do, I should think the matter over very carefully. On one side there's the fact that Rosemary is dead. You can't bring her back to life whatever you do. If the evidence for suicide isn't particularly good, neither is the evidence for murder. Let us say, for the sake of argument, that Rosemary *was* murdered. Do you really wish to rake up the whole thing? It may mean a lot of unpleasant publicity, a lot of washing of dirty linen in public, your wife's love affairs becoming public property—"

George Barton winced. He said violently, "Do you really advise me to let some swine get away with it? That stick Farraday, with his pompous speeches, and his precious career—and all the time, perhaps, a cowardly murderer."

"I only want you to be clear about what it involves."

"I want to get at the truth."

"Very well. In that case, I should go to the police with these letters. They'll probably be able to find out fairly easily who wrote them and if the writer knows anything. Only remember that once you've started them on the trail, you won't be able to call them off."

"I'm not going to the police. That's why I wanted to see you. I'm going to set a trap for the murderer."

"What on earth do you mean?"

"Listen, Race. I'm going to have a party at the Luxembourg. I want you to come. The same people, the Farradays, Anthony Browne, Ruth, Iris, myself. I've got it all worked out."

"What are you going to do?"

George gave a faint laugh.

"That's my secret. It would spoil it if I told anyone beforehand—even you. I want you to come with an unbiased mind—see what happens."

Race leaned forward. His voice was suddenly sharp.

"I don't like it, George. These melodramatic ideas out of books don't work. Go to the police—there's no better body of men. They know how to deal with these problems. They're professionals. Amateur shows in crime aren't advisable."

"That's why I want you there. You're not an amateur."

"My dear fellow. Because I once did work for M.I.5? And, anyway, you propose to keep me in the dark."

"That's necessary."

Race shook his head.

"I'm sorry. I refuse. I don't like your plan and I won't be a party to it. Give it up, George, there's a good fellow."

"I'm not going to give it up. I've got it all worked out."

"Don't be so damned obstinate. I know a bit more about these shows than you do. I don't like the idea. It won't work. It may even be—dangerous. Have you thought of that?"

"It will be dangerous for somebody all right."

Race sighed.

"You don't know what you're doing. Oh, well, don't say I haven't warned you. For the last time I beg you to give up this cracked-brained idea of yours."

George Barton only shook his head.

CHAPTER 5

THE morning of November first dawned wet and gloomy. It was so dark in the dining room of the house in Elvaston Square that they had to have the lights on at breakfast.

Iris, contrary to her habit, had come down instead of having her coffee and toast sent up to her and sat there white and ghostlike, pushing food about her plate. George rustled his *Times* with a nervy hand and at the other end of the table Lucilla Drake wept copiously into a handkerchief.

"I know the dear boy will do something dreadful. He's

so sensitive—and he wouldn't say it was a matter of life and death if it wasn't."

Rustling his paper, George said sharply, "Please don't worry, Lucilla. I've said I'll see to it."

"I know, dear George, you are always so kind. But I do feel any delay might be fatal. All these inquiries you speak of making—they will all take *time.*"

"No, no, we'll hurry them through."

"He says: 'without fail by the second' and tomorrow *is* the second. I should never forgive myself if anything happened to the darling boy."

"It won't." George took a long drink of coffee.

"And there is still that Conversion Loan of mine—"

"Look here, Lucilla, you leave it all to me."

"Don't worry, Aunt Lucilla," put in Iris. "George will be able to arrange it all. After all, this has happened before."

"Not for a long time." ("Three months," said George.) "Not since the poor boy was deceived by those dreadful swindling friends of his on that horrid ranch."

George wiped his moustache on his napkin, got up, patted Mrs. Drake kindly on the back as he made his way out of the room.

"Now do cheer up, my dear. I'll get Ruth to cable right away."

As he went out into the hall, Iris followed him.

"George, don't you think we ought to put off the party tonight? Aunt Lucilla is so upset. Hadn't we better stay at home with her?"

"Certainly not!" George's pink face went purple. "Why should that damned swindling young crook upset our whole lives? It's blackmail—sheer blackmail, that's what it is. If I had my way, he shouldn't get a penny."

"Aunt Lucilla would never agree to that."

"Lucilla's a fool—always has been. These women who have children when they're over forty never seem to learn any sense. Spoil the brats from the cradle by giving them every damned thing they want. If young Victor had once been told to get out of his mess by himself it might have been the making of him. Now don't argue, Iris. I'll get something fixed up before tonight so that Lucilla can go to bed happy. If necessary we'll take her along with us."

"Oh, no, she hates restaurants—and gets so sleepy, poor darling. And she dislikes the heat and the smoky air gives her asthma."

"I know. I wasn't serious. Go and cheer her up, Iris. Tell her everything will be all right."

He turned away and went out of the front door. Iris turned slowly back towards the dining room. The telephone rang and she went to answer it.

"Hullo—who?" Her face changed, its white hopelessness dissolved into pleasure. "Anthony!"

"Anthony himself. I rang you up yesterday but couldn't get you. Have you been putting in a spot of work with George?"

"What do you mean?"

"Well, George was so pressing over this invitation to some party tonight. Quite unlike his usual style of 'hands off my lovely ward!' Absolutely insistent that I should come. I thought perhaps it was the result of some tactful work on your part."

"No—no—it's nothing to do with me."

"A change of heart all on his own?"

"Not exactly. It's—"

"Hullo—have you gone away?"

"No, I'm here."

"You were saying something. What's the matter, darling? I can hear you sighing through the telephone. Is anything the matter?"

"No—nothing. I shall be all right tomorrow. Everything will be all right tomorrow."

"What touching faith. Don't they say 'Tomorrow never comes'?"

"Don't."

"Iris—something *is* the matter?"

"No, nothing. I can't tell you. I promised, you see."

"Tell me, my sweet."

"No—I can't really. Anthony, will you tell *me* something?"

"If I can."

"Were you—ever in love with Rosemary?"

93

A momentary pause and then a laugh.

"So that's it. Yes, Iris, I was a bit in love with Rosemary. She was very lovely, you know. And then one day I was talking to her and I saw you coming down the staircase—and in a minute it was all over, blown away. There was nobody but you in the world. That's the cold sober truth. Don't brood over a thing like that. Even Romeo, you know, had his Rosalind before he was bowled over for good and all by Juliet."

"Thank you, Anthony. I'm glad."

"See you tonight. It's your birthday, isn't it?"

"Actually not for a week—it's my birthday party though."

"You don't sound very enthusiastic about it."

"I'm not."

"I suppose George knows what he's doing, but it seems to me a crazy idea to have it at the same place where—"

"Oh, I've been to the Luxembourg several times since —since Rosemary—I mean, one can't avoid it."

"No, and it's just as well. I've got a birthday present for you, Iris. I hope you'll like it. *Au revoir.*"

He rang off.

Iris went back to Lucilla Drake, to argue, persuade and reassure.

George, on his arrival at his office, sent at once for Ruth Lessing.

His worried frown relaxed a little as she entered, calm and smiling, in her neat black coat and skirt.

"Good morning."

"Good morning, Ruth. Trouble again. Look at this."

She took the cable he held out.

"Victor Drake again!"

"Yes, curse him."

She was silent a minute, holding the cable. A lean brown face wrinkling up around the nose when he laughed. A mocking voice saying "the sort of girl who ought to marry the boss . . ." How vividly it all came back.

She thought, "It might have been yesterday . . ."

George's voice recalled her.

"Wasn't it about a year ago that we shipped him out there?"

She reflected.

"I think so, yes. Actually, I believe it was October 29th."

"What an amazing girl you are. What a memory!"

She thought to herself that she had a better reason for remembering than he knew. It was fresh from his influence that she had listened to Rosemary's careless voice over the phone and decided that she hated her employer's wife.

"I suppose we're lucky," said George, "that he's lasted as long as he has out there. Even if it did cost us fifty pounds last week."

"Three hundred pounds now seems a lot."

"Oh, yes. He won't get as much as that. We'll have to make the usual investigations."

"I'd better communicate with Mr. Ogilvie."

Alexander Ogilvie was their agent in Buenos Aires— a sober, hard-headed Scotsman.

"Yes. Cable at once. Victor's mother is in a state, as usual. Practically hysterical. Makes it very difficult with the party tonight."

"Would you like me to stay with her?"

"No." He negatived the idea emphatically. "No, indeed. You're the one person who's got to be there. I need you, Ruth." He took her hand. "You're too unselfish."

"I'm not unselfish at all."

She smiled and suggested, "Would it be worth trying telephonic communication with Mr. Ogilvie? We might get the whole thing cleared up by tonight."

"A good idea. Well worth the expense."

"I'll get busy at once."

Very gently she disengaged her hand from his and went out.

George dealt with various matters awaiting his attention.

At half past twelve he went out and took a taxi to the Luxembourg.

Charles, the notorious and popular head waiter, came

towards him, bending his stately head and smiling in welcome.

"Good morning, Mr. Barton."

"Good morning, Charles. Everything all right for to-night?"

"I think you will be satisfied, sir."

"The same table?"

"The middle one in the alcove, that is right, is it not?"

"Yes—and you understand about the extra place?"

"It is all arranged."

"And you've got the—the rosemary?"

"Yes, Mr. Barton. I am afraid it won't be very decorative. You wouldn't like some red berries incorporated— or say a few chrysantheumums?"

"No, no, only the rosemary."

"Very good, sir. You would like to see the menu. Giuseppe."

With a flick of the thumb Charles produced a smiling little middle-aged Italian.

"The menu for Mr. Barton."

It was produced.

Oysters, Clear Soup, Sole Luxembourg, Grouse, Poires Hélène, Chicken Livers in Bacon.

George cast an indifferent eye over it.

"Yes, yes, quite all right."

He handed it back. Charles accompanied him to the door.

Sinking his voice a little, he murmured, "May I just mention how appreciative we are, Mr. Barton, that you are—er—coming back to us?"

A smile, rather a ghastly smile, showed on George's face. He said, "We've got to forget the past—can't dwell on the past. All that is over and done with."

"Very true, Mr. Barton. You know how shocked and grieved we were at the time. I'm sure I hope that Mademoiselle will have a very happy birthday party and that everything will be as you like it."

Gracefully bowing, Charles withdrew and darted like an angry dragon-fly on some very inferior grade of waiter who was doing the wrong thing at a table near the window.

George went out with a wry smile on his lips. He was not an imaginative enough man to feel a pang of sympathy for the Luxembourg. It was not, after all, the fault of the Luxembourg that Rosemary had decided to commit suicide there or that someone had decided to murder her there. It had been decidedly hard on the Luxembourg. But like most people with an idea, George thought only of that idea.

He lunched at his club and went afterwards to a Directors' meeting.

On his way back to the office, he put through a phone call to a Maida Vale number from a public call box. He came out with a sigh of relief. Everything was set according to schedule.

He went back to the office.

Ruth came to him at once.

"About Victor Drake."

"Yes?"

"I'm afraid it's rather a bad business. A possibility of criminal prosecution. He's been helping himself to the firm's money over a considerable period."

"Did Ogilvie say so?"

"Yes. I got through to him this morning and he got a call through to us this afternoon ten minutes ago. He says Victor was quite brazen about the whole thing."

"He would be!"

"But he insists that they won't prosecute if the money is refunded. Mr. Ogilvie saw the senior partner and that seems to be correct. The actual sum in question is one hundred and sixty-five pounds."

"So that Master Victor was hoping to pocket a clear hundred and thirty-five on the transaction?"

"I'm afraid so."

"Well, we've scotched that, at any rate," said George with grim satisfaction.

"I told Mr. Ogilvie to go ahead and settle the business. Was that right?"

"Personally I should be delighted to see that young crook go to prison—but one has to think of his mother. A fool—but a dear soul. So Master Victor scores as usual."

"How good you are," said Ruth.

"Me?"

"I think you are the best man in the world."

He was touched. He felt pleased and embarrassed at the same time. On an impulse he picked up her hand and kissed it.

"Dearest Ruth. My dearest and best of friends. What would I have done without you?"

They stood very close together.

She thought, "I could have been happy with him. I could have made him happy. If only—"

He thought, "Shall I take Race's advice? Shall I give it all up? Wouldn't that really be the best thing?"

Indecision hovered over him and passed. He said, "Nine-thirty at the Luxembourg."

CHAPTER 6

THEY had all come.

George breathed a sigh of relief. Up to the last moment he had feared some last minute defection—but they were all here. Stephen Farraday, tall and stiff, a little pompous in manner. Sandra Farraday in a severe black velvet gown wearing emeralds round her neck. The woman had breeding, not a doubt of it. Her manner was completely natural, possibly a little more gracious than usual. Ruth also in black with no ornament save one jewelled clip. Her raven black hair smooth—and lying close to her head, her neck and arms very white—whiter than those of the other women. Ruth was a working girl, she had no long leisured ease in which to acquire sun-tan. His eyes met hers and, as though she saw the anxiety in his, she smiled reassurance. His heart lifted. Loyal Ruth. Beside him Iris was unusually silent. She alone showed consciousness of this being an unusual party. She was pale but in some way it suited her, gave her a grave steadfast beauty. She wore a straight simple frock of leaf green. Anthony Browne came last, and to George's mind, he came with the quick stealthy step of a wild creature—a panther, perhaps, or a leopard. The fellow wasn't really quite civilized.

They were all there—all safe in George's trap. Now, the play could begin . . .

Cocktails were drained. They got up and passed through the open arch into the restaurant proper.

Dancing couples, soft Negro music, deft hurrying waiters.

Charles came forward and smilingly piloted them to their table. It was at the far end of the room, a shallow arched alcove which held three tables—a big one in the middle and two small ones for two people either side of it. A middle-aged sallow foreigner and a blond lovely were at one, a slip of a boy and a girl at the other. The middle table was reserved for the Barton party.

George genially assigned them to their places.

"Sandra, will you sit there, on my right? Browne next to her. Iris, my dear, it's your party. I must have you here next to me, and you beyond her, Farraday. Then you, Ruth—"

He paused—between Ruth and Anthony was a vacant chair—the table had been laid for seven.

"My friend Race may be a bit late. He said we weren't to wait for him. He'll be along sometime. I'd like you all to know him—he's a splendid fellow, knocked about all over the world and can tell you some good yarns."

Iris was conscious of a feeling of anger as she seated herself. George had done it on purpose—separated her from Anthony. Ruth ought to have been sitting where she was, next to her host. So George still disliked and mistrusted Anthony.

She stole a glance across the table. Anthony was frowning. He did not look across at her. Once he directed a sharp sideways glance at the empty chair beside him. He said, "Glad you've got another man, Barton. There's just a chance I may have to go off early. Quite unavoidable. But I ran into a man here I know."

George said smilingly, "Running business into pleasure hours? You're too young for that, Browne. Not that I've ever known exactly what your business is?"

By chance there was a lull in the conversation. Anthony's reply came deliberately and coolly.

"Organized crime, Barton, that's what I always say when I'm asked. Robberies arranged. Larcenies a feature. Families waited upon at their private addresses."

Sandra Farraday laughed as she said, "You're something to do with armaments, aren't you, Mr. Browne? An armament king is always the villain of the piece nowadays."

Iris saw Anthony's eyes momentarily widen in a stare of quick surprise. He said lightly, "You mustn't give me away, Lady Alexandra, it's all very hush-hush. The spies of a foreign power are everywhere. Careless talk."

He shook his head with mock solemnity.

The waiter took away the oyster plates. Stephen asked Iris if she would like to dance.

Soon they were all dancing. The atmosphere lightened.

Presently Iris's turn came to dance with Anthony.

She said, "Mean of George not to let us sit together."

"Kind of him. This way I can look at you all the time across the table."

"You won't really have to go early?"

"I might."

Presently he said, "Did you know that Colonel Race was coming?"

"No, I hadn't the least idea."

"Rather odd, that."

"Do you know him? Oh, yes, you said so the other day."

She added, "What sort of a man is he?"

"Nobody quite knows."

They went back to the table. The evening wore on. Slowly the tension, which had relaxed, seemed to close again. There was an atmosphere of taut nerves about the table. Only the host seemed genial and unconcerned.

Iris saw him glance at his watch.

Suddenly there was a roll of drums—the lights went down. A stage rose in the room. Chairs were pushed a little back, turned sideways. Three men and three girls took the floor, dancing. They were followed by a man who could makes noises. Trains, steam rollers, airplanes, sewing machines, cows coughing. He was a success. Lenny and Flo followed in an exhibition dance which was more of a trapeze act than a dance. More applause. Then another ensemble by the Luxembourg Six. The lights went up.

Everyone blinked.

At the same time a wave of sudden freedom from restraint seemed to pass over the party at the table. It was as though they had been subconsciously expecting something that had failed to happen. For on an earlier occasion the going up of the lights had coincided with the discovery of a dead body lying across the table. It was as though now the past was definitely past—vanished into oblivion. The shadow of a bygone tragedy had lifted.

Sandra turned to Anthony in an animated way. Stephen made an observation to Iris and Ruth leaned forward to join in. Only George sat in his chair staring—staring, his eyes fixed on the empty chair opposite him.

A nudge from Iris recalled him.

"Wake up, George. Come and dance. You haven't danced with me yet."

He roused himself. Smiling at her he lifted his glass.

"We'll drink a toast first—to the young lady whose birthday we're celebrating. Iris Marle, may her shadow never grow less!"

They drank it, laughing, then they all got up to dance, George and Iris, Stephen and Ruth, Anthony and Sandra.

It was a gay jazz melody.

They all came back together, laughing and talking. They sat down.

Then suddenly George leaned forward.

"I've something I want to ask you all. A year ago, more or less, we were here before on an evening that ended tragically. I don't want to recall past sadness, but it's just that I don't want to feel that Rosemary is completely forgotten. I'll ask you to drink to her memory —for remembrance sake."

He raised his glass. Everyone else obediently raised theirs. Their faces were polite masks.

George said, "To Rosemary, for remembrance."

The glasses were raised to their lips. They drank.

There was a pause—then George swayed forward and slumped down in his chair, his hands rising frenziedly to his neck, his face turning purple as he fought for breath.

It took him a minute and a half to die.

BOOK III

IRIS

*"For I thought that the dead had peace
But it is not so . . ."*

CHAPTER I

COLONEL RACE turned into the doorway of New Scotland Yard. He filled in the form that was brought forward and a very few minutes later he was shaking hands with Chief Inspector Kemp in the latter's room.

The two men were well acquainted. Kemp was slightly reminiscent of that grand old veteran, Battle, in type. Indeed, since he worked under Battle for many years, he had perhaps unconsciously copied a good many of the older man's mannerisms. He bore about him the same suggestion of being carved all in one piece—but whereas Battle had suggested some wood such as teak or oak, Chief Inspector Kemp suggested a somewhat more showy wood—mahogany, say, or good old-fashioned rosewood.

"It was good of you to ring us, Colonel," said Kemp. "We shall want all the help we can get on this case."

"It seems to have got into exalted hands," said Race.

Kemp did not make modest disclaimers. He accepted quite simply the indubitable fact that only cases of extreme delicacy, wide publicity or supreme importance came his way. He said seriously, "It's the Kidderminster connection. You can imagine that means careful going."

Race nodded. He had met Lady Alexandra Farraday

several times. One of those quiet women of unassailable postion whom it seems fantastic to associate with sensational publicity. He had heard her speak on public platforms—without eloquence, but clearly and competently, with a good grasp of her subject, and with an excellent delivery.

The kind of woman whose public life was in all the papers, and whose private life was practically non-existent except as a bland domestic background.

Nevertheless, he thought, such women *have* a private life. They know despair, and love, and the agonies of jealousy. They can lose control and risk life itself on a passionate gamble.

He said curiously, "Suppose she 'done it,' Kemp?"

"Lady Alexandra? Do you think she did, sir?"

"I've no idea. But suppose she did. Or her husband—who comes under the Kidderminster mantle."

The steady sea-green eyes of Chief Inspector Kemp looked in an untroubled way into Race's dark ones.

"If either of them did murder, we'll do our level best to hang him or her. *You* know that. There's no fear and no favour for murderers in this country. But we'll have to be absolutely sure of our evidence—the public prosecutor will insist on that."

Race nodded.

Then he said, "Let's have the doings."

"George Barton died of cyanide poisoning—same thing as his wife a year ago. You said you were actually in the restaurant?"

"Yes. Barton had asked me to join his party. I refused. I didn't like what he was doing. I protested against it and urged him, if he had doubts about his wife's death, to go to the proper people—to you."

Kemp nodded and said, "That's what he ought to have done."

"Instead, he persisted in an idea of his own—setting a trap for the murderer. He wouldn't tell me what that trap was. I was uneasy about the whole business—so much so that I went to the Luxembourg last night so as to keep an eye on things. My table, necessarily, was some distance away—I didn't want to be spotted too obviously. Unfortunately I can tell you nothing. I saw nothing in the least suspicious. The waiters and his own party were the only people who approached the table."

"Yes," said Kemp, "it narrows it down, doesn't it? It was one of them or it was the waiter, Giuseppe Balsano. I've got him on the mat again this morning—thought you might like to see him—but I can't believe he had anything to do with it. Been at the Luxembourg for twelve years—good reputation, married, three children, good record behind him. Gets on well with all the clients."

"Which leaves us with the guests."

"Yes. The same party as was present when Mrs. Barton —died."

"What about that business, Kemp?"

"I've been going into it since it seems pretty obvious that the two hang together. Adams handled it. It wasn't what we call a clear case of suicide, but suicide was the most probable solution and in the absence of any direct evidence suggesting murder, one had to let it go as suicide. Couldn't do anything else. We've a good many cases like that in our records, as you know. Suicide with a query mark. The public doesn't know about the query mark—but we keep it in mind. Sometimes we go on quite a bit of hunting about quietly. Sometimes something crops up—sometimes it doesn't. In this case it didn't."

"Until now."

"Until now. Somebody tipped Mr. Barton off to the fact that his wife had been murdered. He got busy on his own—he as good as announced that he was on the right track—whether he was or not I don't know—but the murderer must have thought so—so the murderer gets rattled and bumps off Mr. Barton. That seems the way of it as far as I can see—I hope you agree?"

"Oh, yes—that part of it seems straightforward enough. God knows what the 'trap' was—I noticed that there was an empty chair at the table. Perhaps it was waiting for some unexpected witness. Anyhow it accomplished rather more than it was meant to do. It alarmed the guilty person so much that he or she didn't wait for the trap to be sprung."

"Well," said Kemp, "we've got five suspects. And we've got the first case to go on—Mrs. Barton."

"You're definitely of the opinion now that it was *not* suicide?"

"This murder seems to prove that it wasn't. Though I don't think you could blame us at the time for accepting the suicide theory as the most probable. There was some evidence for it."

"Depression after influenza?"

Kemp's wooden face showed a ripple of a smile.

"That was for the Coroner's court. Agreed with the medical evidence and saved everybody's feelings. That's done every day. And there was a half-finished letter to the sister directing how her personal belongings were to be given away—showed she'd the idea of doing away with herself in her mind. She was depressed all right, I don't doubt, poor lady—but nine times out of ten, with women, it's a love affair. With men it's mostly money worries."

"So you knew Mrs. Barton had a love affair."

"Yes, we soon found that out. It had been discreet—but it didn't take much finding."

"Stephen Farraday?"

"Yes. They used to meet in a little flat out Earl's Court way. It had been going on for over six months. Say they'd had a quarrel—or possibly he was getting tired of her—well, she wouldn't be the first woman to take her life in a fit of desperation."

"By potassium cyanide in a public restaurant?"

"Yes—if she wanted to be dramatic about it—with him looking on and all. Some people have a feeling for the spectacular. From what I could find out she hadn't much feeling for the conventions—all the precautions were on his side."

"Any evidence as to whether his wife knew what was going on?"

"As far as we could learn she knew nothing about it."

"She may have, for all that, Kemp. Not the kind of woman to wear her heart on her sleeve."

"Oh, quite so. Count them both as possibles. She for jealousy. He for his career. Divorce would have dished that. Not that divorce means as much as it used to, but in his case it would have meant the antagonism of the Kidderminster clan."

"What about the secretary girl?"

"She's a possible. Might have been sweet on George Barton. They were pretty thick at the office and there's an idea there that she was keen on him. Actually yesterday afternoon one of the telephone girls was giving an imitation of Barton holding Ruth Lessing's hand and saying he couldn't do without her, and Miss Lessing came out and caught them and sacked the girl there and then— gave her a month's notice and told her to go. Looks as though she was sensitive about it all. Then the sister came into a peck of money—one's got to remember that. Looked a nice kid, but you never can tell. And there was Mrs. Barton's other boy friend."

"I'm rather anxious to hear what you know about him."

Kemp said slowly, "Remarkably little—but what there is isn't too good. His passport's in order. He's an American citizen about whom we can't find out anything, detrimental or otherwise. He came over here, stayed at Claridge's and managed to strike up an acquaintanceship with Lord Dewsbury."

"Confidence man?"

"Might be. Dewsbury seems to have fallen for him— asked him to stay. Rather a critical time just then."

"Armaments," said Race. "There was that trouble about the new tank trials in Dewsbury's works."

"Yes. This fellow Browne represented himself as interested in armaments. It was soon after he'd been up there that they discovered that sabotage business—just in the nick of time. Browne met a good many cronies of Dewsbury's—he seems to have cultivated all the ones who were connected with the armament firms. As a result he's been shown a lot of stuff that in my opinion he ought never to have seen—and in one or two cases there's been serious trouble in the works not long after he's been in the neighbourhood."

"An interesting person, Mr. Anthony Browne."

"Yes. He's got a lot of charm, apparently, and plays it for all he's worth."

"And where did Mrs. Barton come in? George Barton hasn't anything to do with the armament world?"

"No. But they seem to have been fairly intimate. He may have let out something to you. *You* know, Colonel, none better, what a pretty woman can get out of a man."

Race nodded, taking the Chief Inspector's words, as meant, to refer to the Counter-Espionage Department which he had once controlled, but not—as some ignorant person might have thought—to some personal indiscretions of his own.

He said after a minute or two, "Have you had a go at those letters that George Barton received?"

"Yes. Found them in his desk at his house last night. Miss Marle found them for me."

"You know I'm interested in those letters, Kemp. What's the expert opinion on them?"

"Cheap paper, ordinary ink—finger-prints show George Barton and Iris Marle handled them—and a horde of unidentified dabs on the envelope, postal employees, etc. They were printed and the experts say by someone of good education in normal health."

"Good education. Not a servant?"

"Presumably not."

"That makes it more interesting still."

"It means that somebody else had suspicions, at least."

"Someone who didn't go to the police. Someone who was prepared to arouse George's suspicions but who didn't follow the business up. There's something odd there, Kemp. He couldn't have written them himself, could he?"

"He could have. But why?"

"As a preliminary to suicide—a suicide which he intended to look like murder."

"With Stephen Farraday booked for the hangman's rope? It's an idea—but he'd have made quite sure that everything pointed to Farraday as the murderer. As it is we've nothing against Farraday at all."

"What about the cyanide? Was there any container found?"

108

"Yes. A small white paper packet under the table. Traces of cyanide crystals inside. No finger-prints on it. In a detective story, of course, it would be some special kind of paper or folded in some special way. I'd like to give these detective story writers a course of routine work. They'd soon learn how most things are untraceable and nobody ever notices anything anywhere!"

Race smiled.

"Almost too sweeping a statement. Did nobody notice anything last night?"

"Actually that's what I'm starting on today. I took a brief statement from everyone last night and I went back to Elvaston Square with Miss Marle and had a look through Barton's desk and papers. I shall get fuller statements from them all today—also statements from the people sitting at the other two tables in the alcove—" He rustled through some papers—"Yes, here they are. Gerald Tollington, Grenadier Guards, and the Honourable Patricia Brice-Woodworth. Young engaged couple. I'll bet they didn't see anything but each other. And Mr. Pedro Morales—nasty bit of goods from Mexico—even the whites of his eyes are yellow—and Miss Christine Shannon —a gold-digging blond lovely—I'll bet she didn't see anything—dumber than you'd believe possible except where money is concerned. It's a hundred to one chance that any of them saw anything, but I took their names and addresses on the off chance. We'll start off with the waiter chap, Giuseppe. He's here now. I'll have him sent in."

CHAPTER 2

GIUSEPPE BALSANO was a middle-aged man, with a rather monkey-like, intelligent face. He was nervous, but not unduly so. His English was fluent since he had, he explained, been in the country since he was sixteen and had married an English wife.

Kemp treated him sympathetically.

"Now then, Giuseppe, let's hear whether anything more has occurred to you about this."

"It is for me very unpleasant. It is I who serve that table. I who pour out the wine. People will say that I am off my head, that I put poison into the wine glasses. It is not so, but that is what people will say. Already, Mr. Goldstein says it is better that I take a week away from work—so that people do not ask me questions there and point me out. He is a fair man, and just, and he knows it is not my fault, and that I have been there for many years, so he does not dismiss me as some restaurant owners would do. Mr. Charles, too, he has been kind, but all the same it is a great misfortune for me—and it makes me afraid. Have I an enemy, I ask myself?"

"Well," said Kemp at his most wooden, "have you?"

The sad monkey-face twitched into laughter. Giuseppe stretched his arms.

"I? I have not an enemy in the world. Many good friends but no enemies."

Kemp grunted.

"Now about last night. Tell me all about the champagne."

"It was Cliquot 1928—very good and expensive wine. Mr. Barton was like that—he liked good food and drink —the best."

"Had he ordered the wine beforehand?"

"Yes. He had arranged everything with Charles."

"What about the vacant place at the table?"

"That, too, he had arranged for. He told Charles and he told me. A young lady would occupy it later in the evening.

"A young lady?" Race and Kemp looked at each other. "Do you know who the young lady was?"

Giuseppe shook his head.

"No, I know nothing about that. She was to come later, that is all I heard."

"Go on about the wine. How many bottles?"

"Two bottles and a third to be ready if needed. The first bottle was finished quite quickly. The second I open

110

not long before the cabaret. I fill up the glasses and put the bottle in the ice bucket."

"When did you last notice Mr. Barton drinking from his glass?"

"Let me see, when the cabaret was over, they drink the young lady's health. It is her birthday so I understand. Then they go and dance. It is after that, when they come back, that Mr. Barton drinks and in a minute, like *that!* he is dead."

"Had you filled up the glasses during the time they were dancing?"

"No, Monsieur. They were full when they drank to Mademoiselle and they did not drink much, only a few mouthfuls. There was plenty left in the glasses."

"Did anyone—*anyone at all*—come near the table whilst they were dancing?"

"No one at all, sir. I am sure of that."

"Did they all go to dance at the same time?"

"Yes."

"And came back at the same time?"

Giuseppe screwed up his eyes in an effort of memory.

"Mr. Barton he came back first—with the young lady. He was stouter than the rest—he did not dance quite so long, you comprehend. Then came the fair gentleman, Mr. Farraday, and the young lady in black. Lady Alexandra Farraday and the dark gentleman came last."

"You know Mr. Farraday and Lady Alexandra?"

"Yes, sir. I have seen them in the Luxembourg often. They are very distinguished."

"Now, Giuseppe, would you have seen if one of those people had put something in Mr. Barton's glass?"

"That I cannot say, sir. I have my service, the other two tables in the alcove, and two more in the main restaurant. There are dishes to serve. I do not watch Mr. Barton's table. After the cabaret nearly everyone gets up and dances, so at that time I am standing still—and that is why I can be sure that no one approached the table then. But as soon as people sit down, I am at once very busy."

Kemp nodded.

"But I think," Giuseppe continued, "that it would be

111

very difficult to do without being observed. It seems to me that only Mr. Barton himself could do it. But you do not think so, no?"

He looked inquiringly at the police officer.

"So that's your idea, is it?"

"Naturally I know nothing—but I wonder. Just a year ago that beautiful lady, Mrs. Barton, she kills herself. Could it not be that Mr. Barton he grieves so much that he too decides to kill himself the same way? It would be poetic. Of course it is not good for the restaurant—but a gentleman who is going to kill himself would not think of that."

He looked eagerly from one to the other of the two men.

Kemp shook his head.

"I doubt if it's as easy as that," he said.

He asked a few more questions, then Giuseppe was dismissed.

As the door closed behind Giuseppe, Race said:

"I wonder if that's what we are meant to think?"

"Grieving husband kills himself on anniversary of wife's death? Not that it was the anniversary—but near enough."

"It was All Saints' Day," said Race.

"True. Yes, it's possible that that *was* the idea—but if so, whoever it was can't have known about those letters being kept and that Mr. Barton had consulted you and shown them to Iris Marle."

He glanced at his watch.

"I'm due at Kidderminster House at twelve-thirty. We've time before that to go and see those people at the other two tables—some of them at any rate. Come with me, won't you, Colonel?"

CHAPTER 3

MR. MORALES was staying at the Ritz. He was hardly a pretty sight at this hour in the morning, still unshaven, the whites of his eyes bloodshot and with every sign of a severe hang-over.

Mr. Morales was an American subject and spoke a variant of the American language. Though professing himself willing to remember anything he could, his recollections of the previous evening were of the vaguest description.

"Went with Chrissie—that baby is sure hard-boiled! She said it was a good joint. 'Honey pie,' I said, "we'll go just where you say.' It was a classy joint, that I'll admit— and do they know how to charge you! Set me back the best part of thirty dollars. But the band was punk—they just couldn't seem to swing it."

Diverted from his recollections of his own evening, Mr. Morales was pressed to remember the table in the middle of the alcove. Here he was not very helpful.

"Sure there was a table and some people at it. I don't remember what they looked like, though. Didn't take much account of them till the guy there croaked. Thought at first he couldn't hold his liquor. Say now, I remember one of the dames. Dark hair and she had what it takes, I should say."

"You mean the girl in the green velvet dress?"

"No, not that one. She was skinny. This baby was in black with some good curves."

It was Ruth Lessing who had taken Mr. Morales' roving eye.

He wrinkled up his nose appreciatively.

"I watched her dancing—and say, could that baby dance! I gave her the high sign once or twice, but she had a frozen eye—just looked through me in your British way."

Nothing more of value could be extracted from Mr. Morales and he admitted frankly that his alcoholic condition was already well advanced by the time the cabaret was on.

Kemp thanked him and prepared to take his leave.

"I'm sailing for New York tomorrow," said Morales. "You wouldn't," he asked wistfully, "care for me to stay on?"

"Thank you, but I don't think your evidence will be needed at the inquest."

"You see I'm enjoying it right here—and if it was police business the firm couldn't kick. When the police tell you to stay put, you've got to stay put. Maybe I *could* remember something if I thought hard enough."

But Kemp declined to rise to his wistful bait, and he and Race drove to Brook Street where they were greeted by a choleric gentleman, the father of the Honourable Patricia Brice-Woodworth.

General Lord Woodworth received them with a good deal of outspoke comment.

What on earth was the idea of suggesting that his daughter—*his* daughter!—was mixed up in this sort of thing? If a girl couldn't go out with her fiancé to dine in a restaurant without being subjected to annoyance by detectives and Scotland Yard, what was England coming to? She didn't even know these people—what was their name—Hubbard—Barton? Some City fellow or other! Showed you couldn't be too careful where you went—Luxembourg was always supposed to be all right—but apparently this was the second time a thing of this sort had happened there. Gerald must be a fool to have taken Pat there—these young men thought they knew everything. But in any case he wasn't going to have his daughter badgered and bullied and cross-questioned—not without a solicitor's say-so. He'd ring up old Anderson in Lincoln's Inn and ask him—

Here the General paused abruptly and staring at Race said, "Seen you somewhere. Now where—?"

Race's answer was immediate and came with a smile.

"Badderapore. 1923."

"By Jove," said the General. "If it isn't Johnnie Race! What are you doing mixed up in this show?"

Race smiled.

"I was with Chief Inspector Kemp when the question of interviewing your daughter came up. I suggested it would be much pleasanter for her if Inspector Kemp came round here than if she had to come down to Scotland Yard, and I thought I'd come along too."

"Oh—er—well, very decent of you, Race."

"We naturally wanted to upset the young lady as little as possible," put in Chief Inspector Kemp.

But at this moment the door opened and Miss Patricia Brice-Woodworth walked in and took charge of the situation with the coolness and detachment of the very young.

"Hullo," she said. "You're from Scotland Yard, aren't you? About last night? I've been longing for you to come. Is father being tiresome? Now don't, daddy—you know what the doctor said about your blood pressure. Why you want to get into such states about everything, I can't think. I'll just take the Inspectors or Superintendents or whatever they are into my room and I'll send Walters to you with a whisky and soda."

The General had a choleric desire to express himself in several blistering ways at once, but only succeeded in saying, "Old friend of mine, Major Race," at which introduction, Patricia lost interest in Race and bent a beatific smile on Chief Inspector Kemp.

With cool generalship, she shepherded them out of the room and into her own sitting room, firmly shutting her father in his study.

"Poor daddy," she observed. "He *will* fuss. But he's quite easy to manage really."

The conversation then proceeded on most amicable lines but with very little result.

"It's maddening really," said Patricia. "Probably the only chance in my life that I shall ever have of being right on the spot when a murder was done—it is murder, isn't it? The papers were very cautious and vague, but I said to Gerry on the telephone that it must be murder. Think of it, a murder done right close by me and I wasn't even looking!"

The regret in her voice was unmistakable.

It was evident enough that, as the chief Inspector had gloomily prognosticated, the two young people who had got engaged only a week previously had had eyes only for each other.

With the best will in the world, a few personalities were all that Patricia Brice-Woodworth could muster.

"Sandra Farraday was looking very smart, but then she always does. That was a Schiaparelli model she had on."

"You know her?" Race asked.

Patricia shook her head.

"Only by sight. He looks rather a bore, I always think. So pompous, like most politicians."

"Did you know any of the others by sight?"

She shook her head.

"No, I'd never seen any of them before—at least I don't think so. In fact, I don't suppose I should have noticed Sandra Farraday if it hadn't been for the Schiaparelli."

"And you'll find," said Chief Inspector Kemp grimly as they left the house, "that Master Tollington will be exactly the same—only there won't have been even a Skipper—skipper—what—sounds like a sardine—to attract his attention."

"I don't suppose," agreed Race, "that the cut of Stephen Farraday's dress suit will have caused him any heart pangs."

"Oh, well," said the Inspector. "Let's try Christine Shannon. Then we'll have finished with the outside chances."

Miss Shannon was, as Chief Inspector Kemp had stated, a blond lovely. The bleached hair, carefully arranged, swept back from a soft, vacant, babylike countenance. Miss Shannon might be, as Inspector Kemp had affirmed, dumb—but she was eminently easy to look at, and a certain shrewdness in the large baby-blue eyes indicated that her dumbness only extended in intellectual directions and that where horse sense and a knowledge of finance were indicated, Christine Shannon was right on the spot.

She received the two men with the utmost sweetness, pressing drinks upon them and when these were refused, urging cigarettes. Her flat was small and cheaply modernistic.

"I'd just love to be able to help you, Chief Inspector. Do ask me any questions you like."

Kemp led off with a few conventional questions about the bearing and demeanour of the party at the centre table.

At once Christine showed herself to be an unusually keen and shrewd observer.

"The party wasn't going well—you could see that. Stiff as stiff could be. I felt quite sorry for the old boy—the one who was giving it. Going all out he was to try and make things go—and just as nervous as a cat on wires—but all he could do didn't seem to cut any ice. The tall woman he'd got on his right was as stiff as though she'd swallowed the poker and the kid on his left was just mad, you could see, because she wasn't sitting next to the nice-looking dark boy opposite. As for the tall fair fellow next to her, he looked as though his tummy was out of order, ate his food as though he thought it would choke him. The woman next to him was doing her best; she pegged away at him, but she looked rather as though she had the jumps herself."

"You seem to have been able to notice a great deal, Miss Shannon," said Colonel Race.

"I'll let you into a secret. I wasn't being so much amused myself. I'd been out with that gentleman friend of mine three nights running, and was I getting tired of him! He was all out for seeing London—especially what he called the classy spots and I will say for him he wasn't mean. Champagne every time. We went to the Compradour and the Mille Fleurs and finally the Luxembourg, and I'll say he enjoyed himself. In a way it was kind of pathetic. But his conversation wasn't what you'd call interesting. Just long histories of business deals he'd put through in Mexico and most of those I heard three times —and going on to all the dames he'd known and how mad they were about him. A girl gets kind of tired of listening after a while and you'll admit that Pedro is nothing much to look at—so I just concentrated on the eats and let my eyes roam around."

"Well, that's excellent from our point of view, Miss Shannon," said the Chief Inspector. "And I can only hope that you will have seen something that may help us solve our problem."

Christine shook her blond head.

"I've no idea who bumped the old boy off—no idea at all. He just took a drink of champagne, went purple in the face and sort of collapsed."

"Do you remember when he had last drunk from his glass before that?"

The girl reflected.

"Why—yes—it was just after the cabaret. The lights went up and he picked up his glass and said something and the others did it too. Seemed to me it was a toast of some kind."

The Chief Inspector nodded.

"And then?"

"Then the music began and they all got up and went off to dance, pushing their chairs back and laughing. Seemed to get warmed up for the first time. Wonderful what champagne will do for the stickiest parties.

"They all went together—leaving the table empty?"

"Yes."

"And no one touched Mr. Barton's glass?"

"No one at all." Her reply came promptly. "I'm perfectly certain of that."

"And no one—no one at all—came near the table while they were away?"

"No one—except the waiter, of course."

"A waiter? Which waiter?"

"One of the half-fledged ones with an apron, round about sixteen. Not the real waiter. He was an obliging little fellow rather like a monkey—Italian I guess he was."

Chief Inspector Kemp acknowledged this description of Giuseppe Balsano with a nod of the head. "And what did he do, this young waiter? He filled up the glasses?"

Christine shook her head.

"Oh, no. He didn't touch anything on the table. He just picked up an evening bag that one of the girls had dropped when they all got up."

"Whose bag was it?"

Christine took a minute or two to think. Then she said, "That's right. It was the kid's bag—a green and gold thing. The other two women had black bags."

"What did the waiter do with the bag?"

Christine looked surprised.

"He just put it back on the table, that's all."

"You're quite sure he didn't touch any of the glasses?"

"Oh, no. He just popped the bag down very quickly and ran off because one of the real waiters was hissing at him to go somewhere, or get something, and everything was going to be his fault!"

"And that's the only time anyone went near that table?"

"That's right."

"But, of course, someone might have gone to the table without your noticing."

But Christine shook her head very determinedly.

"No, I'm quite sure they didn't. You see Pedro had been called to the telephone and hadn't got back yet, so I had nothing to do but look around and feel bored. I'm pretty good at noticing things and from where I was sitting there wasn't much else to see but the empty table next to us."

Race asked, "Who came back first to the table?"

"The girl in green and the old boy. They sat down and then the fair man and the girl in black came back, and after them the haughty piece of goods and the good-looking dark boy. Some dancer, he was. When they were all back and the waiter was warming up a dish like mad on the spirit lamp, the old boy leaned foward and made a kind of speech and then they all picked up their glasses again. And then it happened." Christine paused and added brightly, "Awful, wasn't it? Of course, I thought it was a stroke. My aunt had a stroke and she went down just like that. Pedro came back just then and I said, 'Look, Pedro, that man's had a stroke.' And all Pedro would say was, 'Just passing out—just passing out—that's all,' which was about what *he* was doing. I had to keep my eye on him. They don't like you passing out at a place like the Luxembourg. That's why I don't like Latins.

When they've drunk too much they're not a bit refined any more—a girl never knows what unpleasantness she may be let in for." She brooded for a moment and then, glancing at a showy looking bracelet on her right wrist, she added, "Still, I must say they're generous enough."

Gently distracting her from the trials and compensations of a girl's existence, Kemp took her through her story once more.

"That's our last chance of outside help gone," he said to Race when they had left Miss Shannon's flat. "And it would have been a good chance if it had come off. That girl's the right kind of witness. Sees things and remembers them accurately. If there had been anything to see, she'd have seen it. So the answer is that there wasn't anything to see. It's incredible. It's a conjuring trick! George Barton drinks champagne and goes and dances. He comes back, drinks from the same glass that no one has touched and hey, presto, it's full of cyanide. It's crazy—I tell you—it couldn't have happened except that it did."

He stopped a minute.

"That waiter. The little boy. Giuseppe never mentioned him. I might look into that. After all, he's the one person who was near the table whilst they were all away dancing. There *might* be something in it."

Race shook his head.

"If he'd put anything in Barton's glass, that girl would have seen him. She's a born observer of detail. Nothing to think about inside her head and so she used her eyes. No, Kemp, there must be some quite simple explanation if only we could get it."

"Yes, there's one. He dropped it in the glass himself."

"I'm beginning to believe that that *is* what happened— that it's the only thing that *can* have happened. But if so, Kemp, I'm convinced he didn't know it was cyanide."

"You mean someone gave it to him? Told him it was for indigestion or blood pressure—something like that?"

"It could be."

"Then who was the someone? Not either of the Farradays."

"That would certainly seem unlikely."

"And I'd say Mr. Anthony Browne is equally unlikely. That leaves us two people—an affectionate sister-in-law—"

"And a devoted secretary."

Kemp looked at him.

"Yes—she could have planted something of the kind on him—I'm due now to go to Kidderminster House— What about you? Going round to see Miss Marle?"

"I think I'll go and see the other one—at the office. Condolences of an old friend. I might take her out to lunch."

"So that *is* what you think?"

"I don't think anything yet. I'm casting about for spoor."

"You ought to see Iris Marle, all the same."

"I'm going to see her—but I'd rather go to the house first when she isn't there. Do you know why, Kemp?"

"I'm sure I couldn't say."

"Because there's someone there who twitters—twitters like a little bird . . . 'A little bird told me'—was a saying of my youth. It's very true, Kemp—these twitterers can tell one a lot if one just lets them—twitter!"

CHAPTER 4

THE two men parted. Race hailed a taxi and was driven to George Barton's office in the city. Chief Inspector Kemp, mindful of his expense account, took a bus to within a stone's throw of Kidderminster House.

The Inspector's face was rather grim as he mounted the steps and pushed the bell. He was, he knew, on difficult ground. The Kidderminster faction had immense political influence and its ramifications spread out like a network throughout the country. Chief Inspector Kemp had full belief in the impartiality of British justice. If Stephen or Alexandra Farraday had been concerned in the death of

Rosemary Barton or in that of George Barton no "pull" or "influence" would enable them to escape the consequences. But if they were guiltless, or the evidence against them was too vague to insure conviction, then the responsible officer must be careful how he trod or he would be liable to get a rap over the knuckles from his superiors. In these circumstances it can be understood that the Chief Inspector did not much relish what lay before him. It seemed to him highly probable that the Kidderminsters, would, as he phrased it to himself, "cut up rough."

Kemp soon found, however, that he had been somewhat naïve in his assumption. Lord Kidderminster was far too experienced a diplomat to resort to crudities.

On stating his business, Chief Inspector Kemp was taken at once by a pontifical butler to a dim, book-lined room at the back of the house where he found Lord Kidderminster and his daughter and son-in-law awaiting him.

Coming forward, Lord Kidderminster shook hands and said courteously, "You are exactly on time, Chief Inspector. May I say that I much appreciate your courtesy in coming here instead of demanding that my daughter and her husband should come to Scotland Yard, which, of course, they would have been quite prepared to do if necessary—that goes without saying—but they appreciate your kindness."

Sandra said in a quiet voice, "Yes, indeed, Inspector."

She was wearing a dress of some soft dark material, and sitting as she was, with the light from the long narrow window behind her, she reminded Kemp of a stained glass figure he had once seen in a cathedral abroad. The long oval of her face and the slight angularity of her shoulders helped the illusion. Saint Somebody-or-other, they had told him—but Lady Alexandra Farraday was no saint—not by a long way. And yet some of these old saints had been funny people from his point of view, not kindly ordinary decent Christian folk, but intolerant, fanatical, cruel to themselves and others.

Stephen Farraday stood close by his wife. His face expressed no emotion whatever. He looked correct and formal, an appointed legislator of the people. The natural man was well buried. But the natural man was there, as the Chief Inspector knew.

Lord Kidderminster was speaking, directing with a good deal of ability the trend of the interview.

"I won't disguise from you, Chief Inspector, that this is a very painful and disagreeable business for us all. This is the second time that my daughter and son-in-law have been connected with a violent death in a public place—the same restaurant and two members of the same family. Publicity of such a kind is always harmful to a man in the public eye. Publicity, of course, cannot be avoided. We all realize that, and both my daughter and Mr. Farraday are anxious to give you all the help they can in the hope that the matter may be cleared up speedily and public interest in it die down."

"Thank you, Lord Kidderminster. I much appreciate the attitude you have taken up. It certainly makes things easier for us."

Sandra Farraday said, "Please ask us any questions you like, Chief Inspector."

"Thank you, Lady Alexandra."

"Just one point, Chief Inspector," said Lord Kidderminster. "You have, of course, your own sources of information and I gather from my friend the Commissioner, that this man Barton's death is regarded as murder rather than suicide, though on the face of it, to the outside public, suicide would seem a more likely explanation. *You* thought it was suicide, didn't you, Sandra, my dear?"

The Gothic figure bowed its head slightly. Sandra said in a thoughtful voice, "It seemed to me so obvious last night. We were there in the same restaurant and actually at the same table where poor Rosemary Barton poisoned herself last year. We have seen something of Mr. Barton during the summer in the country and he has really been very odd—quite unlike himself—and we all thought that his wife's death was preying on his mind. He was very fond of her, you know, and I don't think he ever got over her death. So that the idea of suicide seemed, if not natural, at least possible—whereas I can't imagine why *anyone* should want to murder George Barton."

Stephen Farraday said quickly, "No more can I. Barton

was an excellent fellow. I'm sure he hadn't an enemy in the world."

Chief Inspector Kemp looked at the three inquiring faces turned towards him and reflected a moment before speaking. "Better let 'em have it," he thought to himself.

"What you say is quite correct, I am sure, Lady Alexandra. But you see there are a few things that you probably don't know yet."

Lord Kidderminster interposed quickly, "We mustn't force the Chief Inspector's hand. It is entirely in his discretion what facts he makes public."

"Thanks, m'lord, but there's no reason why I shouldn't explain things a little more clearly. I'll boil it down to this: George Barton, before his death, expressed to two people his belief that his wife had not, as was believed, committed suicide, but instead had been poisoned by some third party. He also thought that he was on the track of that third party, and the dinner and celebration last night, ostensibly in honour of Miss Marle's birthday, were really some part of a plan he had made for finding out the identity of his wife's murderer."

There was a moment's silence—and in that silence Chief Inspector Kemp, who was a sensitive man in spite of his wooden appearance, felt the presence of something that he classified as dismay. It was not apparent on any face, but he could have sworn that it was there.

Lord Kidderminster was the first to recover himself. He said, "But surely—that belief in itself might point to the fact that poor Barton was not quite—er—himself. Brooding over his wife's death might have slightly unhinged him mentally."

"Quite so, Lord Kidderminister, but it at least shows that his frame of mind was definitely not suicidal."

"Yes—yes, I take your point."

And again there was a silence. Then Stephen Farraday said sharply, "But how did Barton get such an idea into his head? After all, Mrs. Barton *did* commit suicide."

Chief Inspector Kemp transferred a placid gaze to him.

"Mr. Barton didn't think so."

Lord Kidderminster interposed.

"But the police were satisfied. There was no suggestion of anything but suicide at the time."

Chief Inspector Kemp said quietly, "The facts were compatible with suicide. There was no evidence that her death was due to any other agency."

He knew that a man of Lord Kidderminster's calibre would seize on the exact meaning of that.

Becoming slightly more official, Kemp said, "I would like to ask you some questions now, if I may, Lady Alexandra?"

"Certainly." She turned her head slightly towards him.

"You had no suspicions at the time of Mrs. Barton's death that it might be murder, not suicide?"

"Certainly not. I was quite sure it was suicide." She added, "I still am."

Kemp let that pass. He said, "Have you received any anonymous letters in the past year, Lady Alexandra?"

The calm of her manner seemed broken by pure astonishment.

"Anonymous letters? Oh, no."

"You're quite sure? Such letters are very unpleasant things and people usually prefer to ignore them, but they may be particularly important in this case, and that is why I want to stress that if you did receive any such letters it is most essential that I should know about them."

"I see. But I can only assure you, Chief Inspector, that I have received nothing of the kind."

"Very well. Now you say Mr. Barton's manner has been odd this summer. In what way?"

She considered a minute.

"Well, he was jumpy, nervous. It seemed difficult for him to focus his attention on what was said to him." She turned her head towards her husband. "Was that how it struck you, Stephen?"

"Yes, I should say that was a very fair description. The man looked physically ill, too. He had lost weight."

"Did you notice any difference in his attitude towards you and your husband? Any lesser cordiality, for instance?"

"No. On the contrary. He had bought a house, you know, quite close to us, and he seemed very grateful for what we were able to do for him—in the way of local introductions, I mean, and all that. Of course, we were only too pleased to do everything we could in that line, both for him and for Iris Marle, who is a charming girl."

"Was the late Mrs. Barton a great friend of yours, Lady Alexandra?"

"No, we were not very intimate." She gave a light laugh. "She was really mostly Stephen's friend. She became interested in politics and he helped to—well, educate her politically—which I'm sure he enjoyed. She was a very charming and attractive woman, you know."

"And you're a very clever one," thought Chief Inspector Kemp to himself, appreciatively. "I wonder how much you know about those two—a good deal I shouldn't wonder."

He went on.

"Mr. Barton never expressed to *you* the view that his wife did not commit suicide?"

"No, indeed. That was why I was so startled just now."

"And Miss Marle? She never talked about her sister's death, either?"

"No."

"Any idea what made George Barton buy a house in the country? Did you or your husband suggest the idea to him?"

"No. It was quite a surprise."

"And his manner to you was always friendly?"

"Very friendly indeed."

"Now what do you know about Mr. Anthony Browne, Lady Alexandra?"

"I really know nothing at all. I have met him occasionally and that is all."

"What about you, Mr. Farraday?"

"I think I probably know less about Browne than my wife does. She at any rate has danced with him. He seems like a likable chap—American, I believe."

"Would you say from observation at the time that he was on special terms of intimacy with Mrs. Barton?"

"I have absolutely no knowledge on that point, Chief Inspector."

"I am simply asking you for your impression, Mr. Farraday."

Stephen frowned.

"They were friendly—that is all I can say."

"And you, Lady Alexandra?"

"Simply my impression, Chief Inspector?"

"Simply your impression."

"Then, for what it is worth, I did form the impression that they knew each other well and were on intimate terms. Simply, you understand, from the way they looked at each other—I have no concrete evidence."

"Ladies often have very good judgment on these matters," said Kemp. The somewhat fatuous smile with which he delivered this remark would have amused Colonel Race if he had been present. "Now, what about Miss Lessing, Lady Alexandra?"

"Miss Lessing, I understand, was Mr. Barton's secretary. I met her for the first time on the evening that Mrs. Barton died. After that I met her once when she was staying down in the country, and again last night."

"If I may ask you another informal question, did you form the impression that she was in love with George Barton?"

"I really haven't the least idea."

"Then we'll come to the events of last night."

He questioned both Stephen and his wife minutely on the course of the tragic evening. He had not hoped for much from this, and all he got was confirmation of what he had already been told. All accounts agreed on the important points—Barton had proposed a toast to Iris, had drunk it and immediately afterwards had got up to dance. They had all left the table together and George and Iris had been the first to return to it. Neither of them had any explanation to offer as to the empty chair except that George Barton had distinctly said that he was expecting a friend of his, a Colonel Race, to occupy it later in the evening—a statement which, as the Inspector knew, could not possibly be the truth. Sandra Farraday said, and her husband agreed, that when the lights went up after the cabaret, George had stared at the empty chair in a peculiar manner and had for some moments seemed so absent-minded as not to hear what was said to him—then he had rallied himself and proposed Iris's health.

The only item that the Chief Inspector could count as an addition to his knowledge, was Sandra's account of her conversation with George at Fairhaven—and his plea that she and her husband would collaborate with him over this party for Iris's sake.

It was a reasonably plausible pretext, the Chief Inspector thought, though not the true one. Closing his note-book in which he had jotted down one or two hieroglyphics, he rose to his feet.

"I'm very grateful to you, my lord, and to Mr. Farraday and Lady Alexandra, for your help and collaboration."

"Will my daughter's presence be required at the inquest?"

"The proceedings will be purely formal on this occasion. Evidence of identification and the medical evidence will be taken and the inquest will then be adjourned for a week. By then," said the Chief Inspector, his tone changing slightly, "we shall, I hope, be further on."

He turned to Stephen Farraday.

"By the way, Mr. Farraday, there are one or two small points where I think you could help me. No need to trouble Lady Alexandra. If you will give me a ring at the Yard, we can settle a time that will suit you. You are, I know, a busy man."

It was pleasantly said, with an air of casualness, but on three pairs of ears the words fell with deliberate meaning.

With an air of friendly co-operation Stephen managed to say, "Certainly, Chief Inspector." Then he looked at his watch and murmured, "I must go along to the House."

When Stephen had hurried off, and the Chief Inspector had likewise departed, Lord Kidderminster turned to his daughter and asked a question with no beating about the bush.

"Had Stephen been having an affair with that woman?"

There was a split second of a pause before his daughter answered.

"Of course not. I should have known about it if he had. And anyway, Stephen's not that kind."

128

"Now, look here, my dear, no good laying your ears back and digging your hoofs in. These things are bound to come out. We want to know where we are in this business."

"Rosemary Barton was a friend of that man, Anthony Browne. They went about everywhere together."

"Well," said Lord Kidderminster slowly, "you should know."

He did not believe his daughter. His face, as he went slowly out of the room, was grey and perplexed. He went upstairs to his wife's sitting room. He had vetoed her presence in the library, knowing too well that her arrogant methods were apt to arouse antagonism, and at this juncture he felt it vital that relations with the official police sould be harmonious.

"Well?" said Lady Kidderminster. "How did it go off?"

"Quite well on the face of it," said Lord Kidderminster slowly. "Kemp is a courteous fellow—very pleasant in his manner—he handled the whole thing with tact—just a little too much tact for my fancy."

"It's serious, then?"

"Yes, it's serious. We should never have let Sandra marry that fellow, Vicky."

"That's what I said."

"Yes—yes . . ." He acknowledged her claim. "You were right—and I was wrong. But, mind you, she would have had him anyway. You can't turn Sandra when her mind is fixed on a thing. Her meeting Farraday was a disaster—a man of whose antecedents and ancestors we know nothing. When a crisis comes, how does one know how a man like that will react?"

"I see," said Lady Kidderminster. "You think we've taken a murderer into the family?"

"I don't know. I don't want to condemn the fellow offhand—but it's what the police think—and they're pretty shrewd. He had an affair with this Barton woman—that's plain enough. Either she committed suicide on his account, or else he— Well, whatever happened, Barton got wise to it and was heading for an exposé and scandal. I suppose Stephen simply couldn't take it—and—"

"Poisoned him?"

"Yes."

Lady Kidderminster shook her head.

"I don't agree with you."

"I hope you're right. But somebody poisoned him."

"If you ask me," said Lady Kidderminster, "Stephen simply wouldn't have the nerve to do a thing like that."

"He's in deadly earnest about his career—he's got great gifts, you know, and the makings of a true statesman. You can't say what anyone will do when they're forced into a corner."

His wife still shook her head.

"I still say he hasn't got the nerve. You want someone who's a gambler and capable of being reckless. I'm afraid, William, I'm horribly afraid."

He stared at her. "Are you suggesting that Sandra— *Sandra*—"

"I hate even to suggest such a thing—but it's no use being cowardly and refusing to face possibilities. She's besotted about that man—she always has been—and there's a queer streak in Sandra. I've never really understood her—but I've always been afraid for her. She'd risk anything—*anything*—for Stephen. Without counting the cost. And if she's been mad enough and wicked enough to do this thing, she's got to be protected."

"Protected? What do you mean—protected?"

"By you. We've got to do something about our own daughter, haven't we? Mercifully you can pull any amount of strings."

Lord Kidderminster was staring at her. Though he had thought he knew his wife's character well, he was nevertheless appalled at the force and courage of her realism—at her refusal to blink at unpalatable facts—and also at her unscrupulousness.

"If my daughter's a murderess, do you suggest that I should use my official position to rescue her from the consequences of her act?"

"Of course," said Lady Kidderminster.

"My dear Vicky! You don't understand! One can't do things like that. It would be a breach of—of honour."

"Rubbish!" said Lady Kidderminster.

They looked at each other—so far divided that neither could see the other's point of view. So might Agamemnon and Clytemnestra have stared at each other with the word Iphigenia on their lips.

"You could bring Government pressure to bear on the police so that the whole thing is dropped and a verdict of suicide brought in. It has been done before—don't pretend."

"That has been when it was a matter of public policy—in the interests of the State. This is a personal and private matter. I doubt very much whether I could do such a thing."

"You can if you have sufficient determination."

Lord Kidderminster flushed angrily.

"If I could, I wouldn't! It would be abusing my public position."

"If Sandra were arrested and tried, wouldn't you employ the best counsel and do everything possible to get her off, however guilty she was?"

"Of couse, of course. That's entirely different. You women never grasp these things."

Lady Kidderminster was silent, unperturbed by the thrust. Sandra was the least dear to her of her children—nevertheless, she was at this moment a mother, and a mother only—willing to defend her young by any means, honourable or dishonourable. She would fight with tooth and claw for Sandra.

"In any case," said Lord Kidderminster, "Sandra will not be charged unless there is an absolutely convincing case against her. And I, for one, refuse to believe that a daughter of mine is a murderess. I'm astonished at you, Vicky, for entertaining such an idea for a moment."

His wife said nothing, and Lord Kidderminster went uneasily out of the room. To think that Vicky—*Vicky*—whom he had known intimately for so many years, should prove to have such unsuspected and really very disturbing depths in her!

CHAPTER 5

RACE found Ruth Lessing busy with papers at a large desk. She was dressed in a black coat and skirt and a white blouse and he was impressed by her quiet, unhurried efficiency. He noticed the dark circles under her eyes and the unhappy set line of her mouth, but her grief, if grief it was, was as well controlled as all her other emotions.

Race explained his visit and she responded at once.

"It is very good of you to come. Of course I know who you are. Mr. Barton was expecting you to join us last night, was he not? I remember his saying so."

"Did he mention that before the evening itself?"

She thought for a moment.

"No. It was when we were actually taking our seats round the table. I remember that I was a little surprised—" She paused and flushed slightly. "Not, of course, at his inviting you. You are an old friend, I know. And you were to have been at the other party a year ago. All I meant was that I was surprised, if you were coming, that Mr. Barton hadn't invited another woman to balance the numbers—but, of course, if you were going to be late and might perhaps not come at all—" She broke off. "How stupid I am. Why go over all these petty things that don't matter? I *am* stupid this morning."

"But you have come to work as usual?"

"Of course." She looked surprised—almost shocked. "It is my job. There is so much to clear up and arrange."

"George always told me how much he relied upon you," said Race gently.

She turned away. He saw her swallow quickly and blink her eyes. Her absence of any display of emotion almost convinced him of her entire innocence. Almost, but not quite. He had met women who were good actresses before now, women whose reddened eyelids and the black circles underneath whose eyes had been due to art and not to natural causes.

Reserving judgment, he said to himself, "At any rate she's a cool customer."

Ruth turned back to the desk and in answer to his last remark she said quietly, "I was with him for many years —it will be seven years next April—and I knew his ways; I think he—trusted me."

"I'm sure of that."

He went on. "It is nearly lunch time. I hoped you would come out and lunch quietly with me somewhere. There is a good deal I would like to say to you."

"Thank you. I should like to very much."

He took her to a small restaurant that he knew of, where the tables were set far apart and where a quiet conversation was possible.

He ordered, and when the waiter had gone he looked across the table at his companion.

She was a good-looking girl, he decided, with her sleek dark head and her firm mouth and chin.

He talked a little on desultory topics until the food was brought, and she followed his lead, showing herself intelligent and sensible.

Presently, after a pause, she said, "You want to talk to me about last night? Please don't hesitate to do so. The whole thing is so incredible that I would like to talk about it. Except that it happened and I saw it happen, I would not have believed it."

"You've seen Chief Inspector Kemp, of course?"

"Yes, last night. He seems intelligent and experienced." She paused. "Was it really *murder,* Colonel Race?"

"Did Kemp tell you so?"

"He didn't volunteer any information, but his questions made it plain enough what he had in mind."

"*Your* opinion as to whether or not it was suicide should be as good as anyone's, Miss Lessing. You knew Barton well and you were with him most of yesterday, I imagine. How did he seem? Much as usual? Or was he disturbed— upset—excited?"

She hesitated.

"It's difficult. He was upset and disturbed—but then there was a reason for that."

She explained the situation that had arisen in regard to Victor Drake and gave a brief sketch of that young man's career.

"Hm," said Race. "The inevitable black sheep. And Barton was upset about him?"

Ruth said slowly, "It's difficult to explain. I knew Mr. Barton so well, you see. He was annoyed and bothered about the business—and I gather Mrs. Drake had been very tearful and upset, as she always was on these occasions—so, of course, he wanted to straighten it all out. But I had the impression—"

"Yes, Miss Lessing? I'm sure your impressions will be accurate."

"Well, then, I fancied that his annoyance was not quite the usual annoyance, if I may put it like that. Because we had had this same business before, in one form or another. Last year Victor Drake was in this country and in trouble, and we had to ship him off to South America, and only last June he cabled home for money. So you see I was familiar with Mr. Barton's reactions. And it seemed to me this time that his annoyance was principally at the cable having arrived at this moment when he was entirely preoccupied with the arrangements for the party he was giving. He seemed so taken up by the preparations for it that he grudged any other preoccupation arising."

"Did it strike you that there was anything odd about this party of his, Miss Lessing?"

"Yes, it did. Mr. Barton was really most peculiar about it. He was excited—like a child might have been."

"Did it occur to you that there might have been a special purpose in such a party?"

"You mean that it was a replica of the party a year ago when Mrs. Barton committed suicide?"

"Yes."

"Frankly, I thought it a most extraordinary idea."

"But George didn't volunteer any explanation—or confide in you in any way?"

She shook her head.

"Tell me, Miss Lessing, has there ever been any doubt in your mind as to Mrs. Barton's having committed suicide?"

She looked astonished.

"Oh, no."

"George Barton didn't tell you that he believed his wife had been murdered?"

She stared at him.

"George believed *that?*"

"I see that is news to you. Yes, Miss Lessing. George had received anonymous letters stating that his wife had not committed suicide but had been killed."

"So that it why he became so odd this summer. I couldn't think what was the matter with him."

"You knew nothing about these anonymous letters?"

"Nothing. Were there many of them?"

"He showed me two."

"And I knew nothing about them!"

There was a note of bitter hurt in her voice.

He watched her for a moment or two, then he said, "Well, Miss Lessing, what do you say? Is it possible, in your opinion, for George to have committed suicide?"

She shook her head.

"No—oh, no."

"But you said he was excited—upset?"

"Yes, but he had been like that for some time. I see why now. And I see why he was so excited about last night's party. He must have had some special idea in his head—he must have hoped that by reproducing the conditions, he would gain some additional knowledge—poor George, he must have been so muddled about it all."

"And what about Rosemary Barton, Miss Lessing? Do you still think her death was suicide?"

She frowned.

"I've never dreamed of its being anything else. It seemed so natural."

"Depression after influenza?"

"Well, rather more than that, perhaps. She was definitely very unhappy. One could see that."

"And guess the cause?"

"Well—yes. At least I did. Of course I may have been wrong. But women like Mrs. Barton are very transparent —they don't trouble to hide their feelings. Mercifully, I don't think Mr. Barton suspected anything. Oh, yes, she was very unhappy. And I know she had a bad headache that night beside being run down with 'flu.'"

"How did you know she had a headache?"

"I heard her telling Lady Alexandra so—in the cloak-room when we were taking off our wraps. She was wishing she had a Cachet Faivre and luckily Lady Alexandra had one with her and gave it to her."

Colonel Race's hand stopped with a glass in mid-air.

"And she took it?"

"Yes."

He put his glass down untasted and looked across the table. The girl looked placid and unaware of any significance in what she had said. But it *was* significant. It meant that Sandra who, from her position at table, would have had the most difficulty in putting anything unseen in Rosemary's glass, had had another opportunity of administering the poison. She could have given it to Rosemary in a cachet. Ordinarily a cachet would take only a few minutes to dissolve, but possibly this had been a special kind of cachet; it might have had a lining of gelatine or some other substance. Or Rosemary might possibly not have swallowed it then but later.

He said abruptly, "Did you see her take it?"

"I beg your pardon?"

He saw by her puzzled face that her mind had gone on elsewhere.

"Did you see Rosemary Barton swallow that cachet?"

Ruth looked a little startled.

"I—well, no, I didn't actually see her. She just thanked Lady Alexandra."

So Rosemary might have slipped the cachet in her bag and then, during the cabaret, with a headache increasing, she might have dropped it into her champagne glass and let it dissolve. Assumption—pure assumption—but a possibility.

Ruth said, "Why do you ask me that?"

Her eyes were suddenly alert, full of questions. He

136

watched, so it seemed to him, her intelligence working. Then she said, "Oh, I see. I see why George took that house down there near the Farradays. And I see why he didn't tell me about those letters. It seemed to me so extraordinary that he hadn't. But, of course, if he believed them, it meant that one of us, one of those five people round the table, must have killed her. It might—it might even have been *me!*"

Race said in a very gentle voice, "Had you any reason for killing Rosemary Barton?"

He thought at first that she hadn't heard the question. She sat so very still with her eyes cast down.

But suddenly, with a sigh, she raised them and looked straight at him.

"It is not the sort of thing one cares to talk about," she said, "but I think you had better know. I was in love with George Barton. I was in love with him before he even met Rosemary. I don't think he ever knew—certainly he didn't care. He was fond of me—very fond of me—but I suppose never in that way. And yet I used to think that I would have made him a good wife—that I could have made him happy. He loved Rosemary, but he wasn't happy with her."

Race said gently, "And you disliked Rosemary?"

"Yes, I did. Oh, she was very lovely and very attractive and could be very charming in her way. She never bothered to be charming to me! I disliked her a good deal. I was shocked when she died—and at the way she died, but I wasn't really sorry. I'm afraid I was rather glad."

She paused.

"Please, shall we talk about something else?"

Race responded quickly.

"I'd like you to tell me exactly, in detail, everything you can remember about yesterday—from the morning onwards—especially anything George did or said."

Ruth replied promptly, going over the events of the morning—George's annoyance over Victor's importunity, her own telephone calls to South America and the arrangements made and George's pleasure when the matter was settled. She then described her arrival at the Luxembourg and George's flurried, excited bearing as host. She carried her narrative up to the final moment of the tragedy. Her account tallied in every respect with those he had already heard.

With a worried frown, Ruth voiced his own perplexity.

"It wasn't suicide—I'm sure it wasn't suicide—but how can it have been murder? I mean, how *can* it have been done? The answer is, it couldn't, not by one of us! Then was it someone who slipped the poison into George's glass while we were away dancing? But if so, who could it have been? It doesn't seem to make sense."

"The evidence is that *no one* went near the table while you were dancing," Race remarked.

"Then it really doesn't make sense! Cyanide doesn't get into a glass by itself!"

"Have you absolutely no idea—no suspicion, even, who might have put the cyanide in the glass? Think back over last night. Is there nothing, no small incident, that awakens your suspicions in any degree, however small?"

He saw her face change, saw for a moment uncertainty come into her eyes. There was a tiny, almost infinitesimal pause before she answered, "Nothing."

But there *had* been something. He was sure of that. Something she had seen or heard or noticed that, for some reason or other, she had decided not to tell.

He did not press her. He knew that with a girl of Ruth's type that would be no good. If, for some reason, she had made up her mind to keep silence, she would not, he felt sure, change her mind.

But there had been *something*. That knowledge cheered him and gave him fresh assurance. It was the first sign of a crevice in the blank wall that confronted him.

He took leave of Ruth after lunch and drove to Elvaston Square, thinking of the woman he had just left.

Was it possible that Ruth Lessing was guilty? On the whole, he was prepossessed in her favour. She had seemed entirely frank and straightforward.

Was she capable of murder? Most people were, if you came to it. Capable, not of murder in general, but of one particular, individual murder. That was what made it so difficult to weed anyone out. There was a certain quality of ruthlessness about that young woman. And

138

she had a motive—or rather a choice of motives. By removing Rosemary she had a very good chance of becoming Mrs. George Barton. Whether it was a question of marrying a rich man, or of marrying the man she had loved, the removal of Rosemary was the first essential.

Race was inclined to think that marrying a rich man was not enough. Ruth Lessing was too cool-headed and cautious to risk her neck for mere comfortable living as a rich man's wife. Love? Perhaps. For all her cool and detached manner, he suspected her of being one of those women who can be kindled to unlikely passion by one particular man. Given love of George, and hate of Rosemary, she might have coolly planned and executed Rosemary's death. The fact that it had gone off without a hitch, and that suicide had been universally accepted without demur, proved her inherent capability.

And then George had received anonymous letters (From whom? Why? That was the teasing vexing problem that never ceased to nag at him.) and had grown suspicious. He had planned a trap. And Ruth had silenced him.

No, that wasn't right. That didn't ring true. That spelled panic—and Ruth Lessing was not the kind of woman who panicked. She had better brains than George and could have avoided any trap that he was likely to set with the greatest of ease.

It looked as though Ruth didn't add up after all.

CHAPTER 6

LUCILLA DRAKE was delighted to see Colonel Race.

The blinds were all down and Lucilla came into the room draped in black and with a handkerchief to her eyes and explained, as she advanced a tremulous hand to meet his, how, of course, she couldn't have seen anyone —anyone at all—except such an old friend of dear, *dear* George's—and it was so dreadful to have no man in the house! Really, without a man in the house one didn't know how to tackle *anything*. Just herself, a poor lonely widow, and Iris, just a helpless young girl, and George had always looked after everything. So kind of dear Colonel Race and really she was so grateful—no idea what they ought to do. Of course, Miss Lessing would attend to all business matters—and the funeral to arrange for—but how about the inquest? And so dreadful having the police—actually in the house—plain clothes, of course, and really very considerate. But she was so bewildered and the whole thing was such an absolute tragedy and didn't Colonel Race think it must be all due to *suggestion* —that was what the psychoanalysts said, wasn't it, that everything is *suggestion?* And poor George at that horrid place, the Luxembourg, and practically the same party and remembering how poor Rosemary had died there— and it must have come over him quite suddenly, only if he'd listened to what she, Lucilla, had said, and taken that excellent tonic of dear Dr. Gaskell's—run down, all the summer—yes, thoroughly run down.

Whereupon, Lucilla herself ran down temporarily, and Race had a chance to speak.

He said how deeply he sympathized and how Mrs. Drake must count upon him in every way.

Whereupon, Lucilla started off again and said it was indeed kind of him, and it was the shock that had been so terrible—here today and gone tomorrow, as it said in the Bible, cometh up like grass and cut down in the evening—only that wasn't quite right, but Colonel Race would know what she meant, and it was so nice to feel there was someone on whom they could rely. Miss Lessing meant well, of course, and was very efficient, but rather an unsympathetic manner and sometimes took things upon herself a little too much, and in her, Lucilla's, opinion, George had always relied upon her *far too much,* and at one time she had been really afraid that he might do something foolish which would have been a great pity and probably she would have bullied him unmercifully once they were married. Of course, she, Lucilla, had seen what was in the wind. Dear Iris was so unworldly, and it was nice, didn't Colonel Race think, for young girls to be unspoiled and simple? Iris had really always been very young for her age and very quiet—one didn't know half the time what she was thinking about. Rosemary being so pretty and so gay had been out a great deal, and Iris had mooned about the house, which wasn't really right for a young girl—they should go to classes —cooking and perhaps dressmaking. It occupied their minds and one never knew when it might come in useful. It had really been a mercy that she, Lucilla, had been free to come and live here after poor Rosemary's death— that horrid "flu," quite an unusual kind of "flu," Dr. Gaskell had said. Such a clever man and such a nice breezy manner.

She had wanted Iris to see him this summer. The girl had looked so white and pulled down. "But really, Colonel Race, I think it was the situation of the house. *Low,* you know, and *damp,* with quite a *miasma* in the evenings." Poor George had gone off and bought it all by himself without asking anyone's advice—such a pity. He had said he wanted it to be a surprise, but really it would have been better if he had taken some older woman's advice. Men knew nothing about houses. George might have realized that she, Lucilla, would have been willing to take any *amount* of trouble. For, after all, what was her life now? Her dear husband dead many years ago, and Victor, her dear boy, far away in the Argentine—she meant Brazil, or was it the Argentine? Such an affectionate, handsome boy.

Colonel Race said he had heard she had a son abroad.

For the next quarter of an hour, he was regaled with a full account of Victor's multitudinous activities. Such a spirited boy, willing to turn his hand to anything—here followed a list of Victor's varied occupations. Never unkind, or bearing malice to anyone. "He's always been unlucky, Colonel Race. He was misjudged by his house master and I consider the authorities at Oxford behaved quite disgracefully. People don't seem to understand that a clever boy with a taste for drawing would think it an excellent joke to imitate someone's handwriting. He did it for the fun of the thing, not the money. But he'd always been a good son to his mother, and he never failed to

141

let her know when he was in trouble which showed, didn't it, that he trusted her? Only it did seem curious, didn't it, that the jobs people found for him so often seemed to take him out of England. She couldn't help feeling that if only he could be given a nice job, in the Bank of England say, he would settle down much better. He might perhaps live a little out of London and have a little car.

It was quite twenty minutes before Colonel Race, having heard all of Victor's perfections, and misfortunes, was able to switch Lucilla from the subject of sons to that of servants.

Yes, it was very true what he said, the old-fashioned type of servant didn't exist any longer. Really the trouble people had nowadays! Not that she ought to complain, for really they had been very lucky. Mrs. Pound, though she had the misfortune to be slightly deaf, was an excellent woman. Her pastry sometimes a little heavy and a tendency to over pepper the soup, but really on the whole most reliable—and economical, too. She had been there ever since George married and she had made no fuss about going to the country this year, though there had been trouble with the others over that and the parlourmaid had left—but that really was all for the best—an impertinent girl who answered back—besides breaking six of the best wine-glasses, not one by one at odd times which might happen to *anybody,* but all at once, which really meant gross carelessness; didn't Colonel Race think so?

"Very careless indeed."

"That is what I told her. And I said to her that I should be obliged to say so in her reference—for I really feel one has a *duty,* Colonel Race. I mean, one should not mislead. Faults should be mentioned as well as good qualities. But the girl was—really—well, quite *insolent* and said that at any rate she hoped that in her next place she wouldn't be in the kind of house where people got bumped off—a dreadful common expression, acquired at the Cinema I believe, and ludicrously inappropriate since poor dear Rosemary took her own life—though not at the time responsible for her actions as the Coroner very rightly pointed out—and that dreadful expression refers, I believe, to gangsters executing each other with Tommy guns. I am so thankful that we have nothing of that kind in England. And so, as I say, I put in her reference that Betty Archdale thoroughly understood her duties as parlourmaid and was sober and honest, but that she was inclined to have too many breakages and was not always respectful in her manner. And personally, if *I* had been Mrs. Rees-Talbot, I should have read between the lines and not engaged her. But people nowadays just jump at anything they can get, and will sometimes take a girl who has only stayed her month in three places running."

Whilst Mrs. Drake paused to take breath, Colonel Race asked quickly whether that was Mrs. Richard Rees-Talbot. If so, he had known her, he said, in India.

"I really couldn't say. Cadogan Square was the address."

"Then it *is* my friend."

Lucilla said that the world was such a small place, wasn't it? And that there were no friends like old friends. Friendship was a wonderful thing. She had always thought it had been so romantic about Viola and Paul. Dear Viola, she had been a lovely girl, and so many men in love with her, but, oh, dear, Colonel Race wouldn't even know who she was talking about. One did so tend to re-live the past.

Colonel Race begged her to go on and in return for his politeness received the life history of Hector Marle, of his up-bringing by his sister, of his peculiarities and his weaknesses and finally, when Colonel Race had almost forgotten her, of his marriage to the beautiful Viola. "She was an orphan, you know, and a ward in Chancery." He heard how Paul Bennett, conquering his disappointment at Viola's refusal, had transformed himself from lover to family friend, of his fondness for his godchild, Rosemary, and of his death and the terms of his will. "Which I have always felt *most* romantic—such an enormous fortune! Not, of course, that money is everything—no, indeed. One has only to think of poor Rosemary's tragic death. And even dear Iris I am not quite happy about!"

Race gave her an inquiring look.

"I find the responsibility most worrying. The fact that she is a great heiress is, of course, well known. I keep a very sharp eye on the undesirable type of young man, but what can one do, Colonel Race? One can't look after girls nowadays as one used to do. Iris has friends I know next to nothing about. 'Ask them to the house, dear,' is what I always say—but I gather that some of these young men simply will *not* be brought. Poor George was worried, too. About a young man called Browne. I myself have never seen him, but it seems that he and Iris have been seeing a good deal of each other. And one does feel that she could do better. George didn't like him—I'm quite sure of that. And I always think, Colonel Race, that men are much better judges of other men. I remember thinking Colonel Pusey, one of our churchwardens, such a charming man, but my husband always preserved a very distant attitude towards him and enjoined on me to do the same—and sure enough, one Sunday when he was handing around the offertory plate, he fell right down—completely intoxicated, it seems. And, of course, afterwards—one always hears these things *afterwards,* so much better if one heard them *before*—we found out that dozens of empty brandy bottles were taken out of the house every week! It was very sad really, because he was truly religious, though inclined to be Evangelical in his views. He and my husband had a terrific battle over the details of the service on All Saints' Day. Oh, dear, and it's All Souls' Day today—November second. Dear, dear, to think of it and yesterday All Saints'."

A faint sound made Race look over Lucilla's head at the open doorway. He had seen Iris before—at Little Priors. Nevertheless, he felt that he was seeing her now for the first time. He was struck by the extraordinary tension behind her stillness and her wide eyes met his with something in their expression that he felt he ought to recognize, yet failed to do so.

In her turn, Lucilla Drake turned her head.

"Iris, dear, I didn't hear you come in. You know Colonel Race? He is being so very kind."

Iris came and shook hands with him gravely; the black

144

dress she wore made her look thinner and paler than he remembered her.

"I came to see if I could be of any help to you," said Race.

"Thank you. That was kind of you."

She spoke mechanically, without emotion.

She had had a bad shock, that was evident, and was still suffering from the effects of it. But had she been so fond of George that his death could affect her so powerfully?

She turned her eyes to her aunt and Race realized that they were watchful eyes. She said, "What were you talking about—just now, as I came in?"

Lucilla became pink and flustered. Race guessed that she was anxious to avoid any mention of the young man, Anthony Browne. She exclaimed, "Now, let me see—oh, yes, All Souls' Day—and yesterday being All Saints'. All Saints'—that seems to be such an *odd* thing—one of those coincidences one never believes in in real life."

"Do you mean," said Iris, "that Rosemary came back yesterday to fetch George?"

Lucilla gave a little scream.

"Iris, dear, don't. What a terrible thought—so un-Christian."

"Why un-Christian? It's the Day of the Dead. In Paris people used to go and put flowers on the graves."

"Oh, I know, dear, but then they were Catholics, weren't they?"

A faint smile twisted Iris's lips. Then she said directly, "I thought, perhaps, you were talking of Anthony—Anthony Browne."

"Well," Lucilla's twitter became very high and bird-like, "as a matter of fact we did just *mention* him. I happened to say, you know, that we know *nothing* about him—"

Iris interruped, her voice hard, "Why should you know anything about him?"

"No, dear, of course not. At least, I mean, well, it would be rather nicer, wouldn't it, if we did?"

"You'll have every chance of doing so in the future," said Iris, "because I'm going to marry him."

"Oh, Iris!" It was halfway between a wail and a bleat. "You mustn't do anything rash—I mean, nothing can be settled at present."

"It *is* settled, Aunt Lucilla."

"No, dear, one can't talk about things like marriage when the funeral hasn't even taken place yet. It wouldn't be decent. And this dreadful inquest and everything. And really, Iris, I don't think dear George would have approved. He didn't like this Mr. Browne."

"No," said Iris, "George wouldn't have liked it and he didn't like Anthony, but that doesn't make any difference. It's my life, not George's—and anyway, George is dead . . ."

Mrs. Drake gave another wail.

"Iris, Iris! What has come over you? Really that was a most unfeeling thing to say."

"I'm sorry, Aunt Lucilla." The girl spoke wearily. "I know it must have sounded like that but I didn't mean it that way. I only meant that George is at peace somewhere and hasn't got to worry about me and my future any more. I must decide things for myself."

"Nonsense, dear, nothing can be decided at a time like this—it would be most unfitting. The question simply doesn't arise."

"But it has arisen. Anthony asked me to marry him before we left Little Priors. He wanted me to come up to London and marry him the next day without telling anyone. I wish now that I had."

"Surely that was a very curious request," said Colonel Race gently.

She turned defiant eyes to him.

"No, it wasn't. It would have saved a lot of fuss. Why couldn't I trust him? He asked me to trust him and I didn't. Anyway, I'll marry him now as soon as he likes."

Lucilla burst out in a stream of incoherent protest. Her plump cheeks quivered and her eyes filled.

Colonel Race took rapid charge of the situation.

"Miss Marle, might I have a word with you before I go? On a strictly business matter?"

Rather startled, the girl murmured, "Yes," and found

146

herself moving to the door. As she passed through, Race took a couple of strides back to Mrs. Drake.

"Don't upset yourself, Mrs. Drake. Least said, you know, soonest mended. We'll see what we can do."

Leaving her slightly comforted, he followed Iris, who led him across the hall and into a small room giving out on the back of the house where a melancholy plane tree was shedding its last leaves.

Race spoke in a business-like tone.

"All I had to say, Miss Marle, was that Chief Inspector Kemp is a personal friend of mind, and that I am sure you will find him most helpful and kindly. His duty is an unpleasant one, but I'm sure he will do it with the utmost consideration possible."

She looked at him for a moment or two without speaking, then she said abruptly, "Why didn't you come and join us last night as George expected you to do?"

He shook his head.

"George didn't expect me."

"But he said he did."

"He may have said so, but it wasn't true. George knew perfectly well that I wasn't coming."

She said, "But that empty chair . . . Who was it for?"

"Not for me."

Her eyes half closed and her face went very white.

She whispered, "It was for Rosemary . . . I see . . . It was for Rosemary . . ."

He thought she was going to fall. He came quickly to her and steadied her, then forced her to sit down.

"Take it easy . . ."

She said in a low breathless voice, "I'm all right . . . But I don't know what to do . . . I don't know what to do."

"Can I help you?"

She raised her eyes to his face. They were wistful and sombre.

Then she said, "I must get things clear. I must get them"—she made a groping gesture with her hands—"in sequence. First of all, George believed Rosemary didn't kill herself—but was killed. He believed that because of those letters. Colonel Race, who wrote those letters?"

"I don't know. Nobody knows. Have you yourself any idea?"

"I simply can't imagine. Anyway, George believed what they said, and he arranged this party last night, and he had an empty chair and it was All Saints' Day . . . that's the Day of the Dead—it was a day when Rosemary's spirit could have come back and—and told him the truth."

"You mustn't be too imaginative."

"But I've felt her myself—felt her quite near sometimes —I'm her sister—and I think she's trying to tell me something."

"Take it easy, Iris."

"I *must* talk about it. George drank Rosemary's health and he—died. Perhaps—she came and took him."

"The spirits of the dead don't put potassium cyanide in a champagne glass, my dear."

The words seemed to restore her balance. She said in a more normal tone, "But it's so incredible. George was killed—yes, *killed*. That's what the police think and it must be true, because there isn't any other alternative. But it doesn't make sense."

"Don't you think it does? If Rosemary was killed, and George was beginning to suspect by whom—"

She interrupted him.

"Yes, but Rosemary *wasn't* killed. That's why it doesn't make sense. George believed those stupid letters partly because depression after influenza isn't a very convincing reason for killing yourself. But Rosemary *had* a reason. Look, I'll show you."

She ran out of the room and returned a few moments later with a folded letter in her hand. She thrust it on him.

"Read it. See for yourself."

He unfolded the slightly crumpled sheet.

"Leopard darling—"

He read it twice before handing it back.

The girl said eagerly, "You see? She was unhappy— broken-hearted. She didn't want to go on living."

"Do you know to whom that letter was written?"

Iris nodded.

"Stephen Farraday. It wasn't Anthony. She was in love with Stephen and he was cruel to her. So she took the stuff with her to the restaurant and drank it there where he could see her die. Perhaps she hoped he'd be sorry then."

Race nodded thoughtfully, but said nothing. After a moment or two he said, "When did you find this?"

"About six months ago. It was in the pocket of an old dressing-gown."

"You didn't show it to George?"

Iris cried passionately, "How could I? How could I? Rosemary was my sister. How could I give her away to George? He was so sure that she loved him. How could I show him this after she was dead? He'd got it all wrong, but I couldn't tell *him* so. But what I want to know is, what am I to do *now?* I've shown it to you because you were George's friend. Has Inspector Kemp got to see it?"

"Yes. Kemp must have it. It's evidence, you see."

"But then they'll—they might read it out in court?"

"Not necessarily. That doesn't follow. It's George's death that is being investigated. Nothing will be made public that is not strictly relevant. You had better let me take this now."

"Very well."

She went with him to the front door. As he opened it she said abruptly, "It does show, doesn't it, that Rosemary's death *was* suicide?"

Race said, "It certainly shows that she had a motive for taking her own life."

She gave a deep sigh. He went down the steps. Glancing back once, he saw her standing framed in the open doorway, watching him walk away across the Square.

CHAPTER 7

MARY REES-TALBOT greeted Colonel Race with a positive shriek of unbelief.

"My dear, I haven't seen you since you disappeared so mysteriously from Allahabad that time. And why are you here now? It isn't to see me, I'm quite sure. You never pay social calls. Come on now, own up, you needn't be diplomatic about it."

"Diplomatic methods would be a waste of time with you, Mary. I always have appreciated your X-ray mind."

"Cut the cackle and come to the horses, my pet."

Race smiled.

"Is the maid who let me in Betty Archdale?" he inquired.

"So that's it! Now, don't tell me that that girl, a pure Cockney if ever there was one, is a well known European spy, because I simply don't believe it."

"No, no, nothing of the kind."

"And don't tell me she's one of our Counter-Espionage either, because I don't believe that."

"Quite right. The girl is simply a parlourmaid."

"And since when have you been interested in simple parlourmaids—not that Betty is simple—an artful dodger is more like it."

"I think," said Colonel Race, "that she might be able to tell me something."

"If you asked her nicely? I shouldn't be surprised if you're right. She has the close-to-the-door-when-there's-anything-interesting-going-on technique very highly developed. What does M. do?"

"M. very kindly offers me a drink and rings for Betty and orders it."

"And when Betty brings it?"

"By then M. has very kindly gone away."

"To do some listening outside the door herself?"

"If she likes."

"And after that I shall be bursting with Inside Information about the latest European crisis?"

"I'm afraid not. There is no political situation involved in this."

"What a disappointment! All right. I'll play!"

When Betty Archdale returned, with a salver and the drink upon it, Mrs. Rees-Talbot was standing by the far door into her own sitting room.

"Colonel Race has some questions to ask you," she said, and went out.

Betty turned her impudent eyes on the tall, grey-haired soldier with some alarm in their depths. He took the glass from the tray and smiled.

"Seen the papers today?" he asked.

"Yes, sir." Betty eyed him warily.

"Did you see that Mr. George Barton died last night at the Luxembourg restaurant?"

"Oh, yes, sir." Betty's eyes sparkled with the pleasure of public disaster. "Wasn't it dreadful?"

"You were in service there, weren't you?"

"Yes, sir. I left last winter, soon after Mrs. Barton died."

"She died at the Luxembourg, too."

Betty nodded. "Sort of funny, that, isn't it, sir?"

Race did not think it funny, but he knew what the words were intended to convey. He said gravely, "I see you've got brains. You can put two and two together."

Betty clasped her hands and cast discretion to the winds.

"Was he done in, too? The papers didn't say exactly."

She gave him a quick look out of the corner of her eye. Ever so old, she thought, but he's nice-looking. That quiet kind. A real gentleman. Sort of gentleman who'd have given you a gold sovereign when he was young. Funny, I don't even know what a sovereign looks like! What's he after, exactly?

She said demurely, "Yes, sir."

"But perhaps you never thought it *was* suicide?"

"Well, no, sir. I didn't—not really."

"That's very interesting—very interesting indeed. Why didn't you think so?"

She hesitated; her fingers began pleating her apron.

151

"Please tell me. It may be very important."

So nicely he said that, so gravely. Made you feel important and as though you wanted to help him. And anyway, she *had* been smart over Rosemary Barton's death. Never been taken in, she hadn't!

"She was done in, sir, wasn't she?"

"It seems possible that it may be so. But how did you come to think so?"

"Well." Betty hesitated. "It was something I heard one day."

"Yes?"

His tone was quietly encouraging.

"The door wasn't shut or anything. I mean, I'd never go and listen at a door. I don't like that sort of thing," said Betty virtuously. "But I was going through the hall to the dining room and carrying the silver on a tray and they were speaking quite loud. Saying something she was —Mrs. Barton I mean—about Anthony Browne not being his name. And then he got really nasty, Mr. Browne did. I wouldn't have thought he had it in him—so nice-looking and so pleasant spoken as he was as a rule. Said something about carving up her face—ooh!—and then he said if she didn't do what he told her he'd bump her off. Just like that! I didn't hear any more because Miss Iris was coming down the stairs, and, of course, I didn't think very much of it at the time, but after there was all the fuss about her committing suicide at that party and I heard he'd been there at the time—well, it gave me shivers all down my back—it did indeed!"

"But you didn't say anything?"

The girl shook her head.

"I didn't want to get mixed up with the police—and anyway, I didn't know anything—not really. And perhaps if I had said anything I'd have been bumped off too. Or taken for a ride as they call it."

"I see." Race paused a moment and then said in his gentlest voice, "So you just wrote an anonymous letter to Mr. George Barton?"

She stared at him. He detected no uneasy guilt—nothing but pure astonishment.

"Me? Write to Mr. Barton? Never."

"Now don't be afraid to tell about it. It was really a very good idea. It warned him without your having to give yourself away. It was very clever of you."

"But I didn't, sir. I never thought of such a thing. You mean write to Mr. Barton and say that his wife had been done in? Why, the idea never came into my head!"

She was so earnest in her denial that, in spite of himself, Race was shaken. But it all fitted in so well—it could all be explained so naturally if only the girl had written the letters. But she persisted in her denials, not vehemently nor uneasily, but soberly and without undue protestation. He found himself reluctantly believing her.

He shifted his ground.

"Whom did you tell about this?"

She shook her head.

"I didn't tell anyone. I'll tell you honest, sir, I was scared. I thought I'd better keep my mouth shut. I tried to forget it. I only brought it up once—that was when I gave Mrs. Drake my notice—fussing terribly she'd been, more than a girl could stand, and now wanting me to go and bury myself in the dead of the country and not even a bus route! And then she turned nasty about my reference, saying I broke things, and I said, sarcastic like, that at any rate I'd find a place where people didn't get bumped off—and I felt scared when I'd said it, but she didn't pay any real attention. Perhaps I ought to have spoken out at the time, but I couldn't really tell. I mean, the whole thing might have been a joke. People do say all sorts of things, and Mr. Browne was ever so nice really, and quite a one for joking, so I couldn't tell, sir, could I?"

Race agreed that she couldn't. Then he said, "Mrs. Barton spoke of Browne not being his real name. Did she mention what his real name was?"

"Yes, she did. Because he said, 'Forget about Tony'—now what was it? Tony something . . . Reminded me of the cherry jam Cook had been making."

"Tony Cheriton? Cherable?"

She shook her head.

"More of a fancy name than that. Began with an M. And sounded foreign."

"Don't worry. It will come back to you, perhaps. If so, let me know. Here is my card with my address. If you remember the name write to me to that address."

He handed her the card and a treasury note.

"I will, sir, thank you, sir."

A gentleman, she thought, as she ran downstairs. A pound note, not ten shillings. It must have been nice when there were gold sovereigns. . . .

Mary Rees-Talbot came back into the room.

"Well, successful?"

"Yes, but there's still one snag to surmount. Can your ingenuity help me? Can you think of a name that would remind you of cherry jam?"

"What an extraordinary proposition."

"Think, Mary. I'm not a domestic man. Concentrate on jam making, cherry jam in particular."

"One doesn't often make cherry jam."

"Why not?"

"Well, it's inclined to go sugary—unless you use cooking cherries, morello cherries."

Race gave an exclamation.

"That's it—I bet that's it. Good-bye, Mary, I'm endlessly grateful. Do you mind if I ring that bell so that the girl comes and shows me out?"

Mrs. Ress-Talbot called after him as he hurried out of the room, "Of all the ungrateful wretches! Aren't you going to tell me what it's all about?"

He called back, "I'll come and tell you the whole story later."

"Sez you," murmured Mrs. Rees-Talbot.

Downstairs, Betty waited with Race's hat and stick.

He thanked her and passed out. On the doorstep he paused.

"By the way," he said, "was that name Morelli?"

Betty's face lighted up.

"Quite right, sir. That was it. Tony Morelli, that's the name he told her to forget. And he said he'd been in prison, too."

Race walked down the steps smiling.

From the nearest call box he put through a call to Kemp.

Their interchange was brief but satisfactory. Kemp said, "I'll send off a cable at once. We ought to hear by return. I must say it will be a great relief if you're right."

"I think I'm right. The sequence is pretty clear."

CHAPTER 8

INSPECTOR KEMP was not in a very good humour.

For the last half hour he had been interviewing a frightened white rabbit of sixteen who, by virtue of his uncle Charles' great position, was aspiring to be a waiter of the class required by the Luxembourg. In the meantime, he was one of six harried underlings who ran about with aprons round their waists to distinguish them from the superior article, and whose duty it was to bear the blame for everything, fetch and carry, provide rolls and pats of butter and be continually and unceasingly hissed at in French, Italian and occasionally English. Charles, as befitted a great man, so far from showing favour to a blood relation, hissed, cursed and swore at him even more than he did the others. Nevertheless, Pierre aspired in his heart to be no less than the Head Waiter of a chic restaurant himself one day in the far future.

At the moment, however, his career had received a check, and he gathered that he was suspected of no less than murder.

Kemp turned the lad inside out and disgustedly convinced himself that the boy had done no less and no more than what he had said—namely, picked up a lady's bag from the floor and replaced it by her plate.

"It is as I am hurrying with the sauce to M. Robert and already he is impatient, and the young lady sweeps it off the table, and then I hurry on, for already M. Robert he is making the signs frantically to me. That is all, Monsieur."

And that was all. Kemp disgustedly let him go, feeling strongly tempted to add, "But don't let me catch you doing that sort of thing again."

Sergeant Pollock made a distraction by announcing that they had telephoned up to say that a young lady was asking for him, or rather, for the officer in charge of the Luxembourg case.

"Who is she?"

"Her name is Miss Chloe West."

"Let's have her up," said Kemp resignedly. "I can give her ten minutes. Mr. Farraday's due after that. Oh, well, won't do any harm to keep *him* waiting a few minutes. Makes them jittery, that does."

When Miss Chloe West walked into the room, Kemp was at once assailed by the impression that he recognized her. But a minute later he abandoned that impression. No, he had never seen this girl before, he was sure of that. Nevertheless, the vague, haunting sense of familiarity remained to plague him.

Miss West was about twenty-five, tall, brown-haired and very pretty. Her voice was rather conscious of its diction and she seemed decidedly nervous.

"Well, Miss West, what can I do for you?"

Kemp spoke briskly.

"I read in the paper about the Luxembourg—the man who died there."

"Mr. George Barton? Yes? Did you know him?"

"Well, no, not exactly. I mean I didn't really *know* him."

Kemp looked at her carefully and discarded his first deduction.

Chloe West was looking extremely refined and virtuous—severely so. He said pleasantly, "Can I have your exact name and addresss first please, so that we know where we are?"

"Chloe Elizabeth West, 15, Merryvale Court, Maida Vale. I'm an actress."

Kemp looked at her again out of the corner of his eye, and decided that that was what she really was. Repertory, he fancied—in spite of her looks she was the earnest kind.

"Yes, Miss West."

"When I read about Mr. Barton's death and that the—the police were inquiring into it, I thought perhaps I ought to come and tell you something. I spoke to my friend about it and she seemed to think so. I don't suppose it's really anything to do with it, but—" Miss West paused.

"We'll be the judge of that," said Kemp pleasantly. "Just tell me about it."

"I'm not acting just at the moment," explained Miss West.

Inspector Kemp nearly said "Resting" to show that he knew the proper terms, but restrained himself.

"But my name is down at the agencies and my picture in *Spotlight* . . . That, I understand, is where Mr. Barton saw it. He got into touch with me and explained what he wanted me to do."

"Yes?"

"He told me he was having a dinner party at the Luxembourg and that he wanted to spring a surprise on his guests. He showed me a photograph and told me that he wanted me to make up as the original. I was very much the same colouring, he said."

Illumination flashed across Kemp's mind. The photograph of Rosemary he had seen on the desk in George's room in Elvaston Square. That was who the girl had reminded him of. She *was* like Rosemary Barton—not perhaps startlingly so—but the general type and cast of features were the same.

"He also brought me a dress to wear—I've brought it with me. A greyish green silk. I was to do my hair like the photograph (it was a coloured one) and accentuate the resemblance with make-up. Then I was to come to the Luxembourg and go into the restaurant during the first cabaret show and sit down at Mr. Barton's table where there would be a vacant place. He took me to lunch there and showed me where the table would be."

"And why didn't you keep the appointment, Miss West?"

"Because about eight o'clock that night—someone—Mr. Barton—rang up and said the whole thing had been put off. He said he'd let me know next day when it was

157

coming off. Then, the next morning, I saw his death notice in the paper."

"And very sensibly you came along to us," said Kemp pleasantly. "Well, thank you very much, Miss West. You've cleared up one mystery—the mystery of the vacant place. By the way, you said just now—'someone'—and then, 'Mr. Barton.' Why is that?"

"Because at first I didn't think it *was* Mr. Barton. His voice sounded different."

"It was a man's voice?"

"Oh, yes, I think so—at least—it was rather husky as though he had a cold."

"And that's all he said?"

"That's all."

Kemp questioned her a little longer, but got no further. When she had gone, he said to the Sergeant, "So that was George Barton's famous 'plan.' I see now why they all said he stared at the empty chair after the cabaret and looked queer and absent-minded. His precious plan had gone wrong."

"You don't think it was he who put her off?"

"Not on your life. And I'm not so sure it was a man's voice, either. Huskiness is a good disguise through the telephone. Oh, well, we're getting on. Send in Mr. Farraday if he's here."

CHAPTER 9

OUTWARDLY cool and unperturbed, Stephen Farraday had turned into New Scotland Yard full of inner shrinking. An intolerable weight burdened his spirits. It had seemed that morning as though things were going so well. Why had Inspector Kemp asked for his presence here with such significance? What did he know or suspect? It *could* be only vague suspicion. The thing to do was to keep one's head and admit nothing.

He felt strangely bereft and lonely without Sandra. It

was as though when they two faced a peril together it lost half its terrors. Together, they had strength, courage, power. Alone, he was nothing, less than nothing. And Sandra—did she feel the same? Was she sitting now in Kidderminster House, silent, reserved, proud, and inwardly feeling horribly vulnerable?

Inspector Kemp received him pleasantly but gravely. There was a uniformed man sitting at a table with a pencil and a pad of paper. Having asked Stephen to sit down, Kemp spoke in a strongly formal manner.

"I propose, Mr. Farraday, to take a statement from you. That statement will be written down and you will be asked to read it over and sign it before you leave. At the same time it is my duty to tell you that you are at liberty to refuse to make such a statement and that you are entitled to have your solicitor present if you so desire."

Stephen was taken aback but did not show it. He forced a wintry smile.

"That sounds very formidable, Chief Inspector."

"We like everything to be clearly understood, Mr. Farraday."

"Anything I say may be used against me, is that it?"

"We don't use the word against. Anything you say will be liable to be used in evidence."

Stephen said quietly, "I understand, but I cannot imagine, Inspector, why you should need any further statement from me. You heard all I had to say this morning."

"That was a rather informal session—useful as a preliminary starting-off point. And also, Mr. Farraday, there are certain facts which I imagined you would prefer to discuss with me here. Anything irrelevant to the case we try to be as discreet about as is compatible with the attainment of justice. I dare say you understand what I am driving at?"

"I'm afraid I don't."

Chief Inspector Kemp sighed.

"Just this. You were on very intimate terms with the late Mrs. Rosemary Barton—"

Stephen interrupted him.

"Who says so?"

Kemp leaned forward and took a typewritten document from his desk.

"This is a copy of a letter found amongst the late Mrs. Barton's belongings. The original is filed here and was handed to us by Miss Iris Marle, who recognized the writing as that of her sister."

Stephen read:

"Leopard darling—"

A wave of sickness passed over him. Rosemary's voice . . . speaking—pleading . . . Would the past never die—never consent to be buried?

He pulled himself together and looked at Kemp.

"You may be correct in thinking Mrs. Barton wrote this letter—but there is nothing to indicate that it was written to me."

"Do you deny that you paid the rent of 21 Malland Mansions, Earl's Court?"

So they knew. He wondered if they had known all the time. He shrugged his shoulders.

"You seem very well informed. May I ask why my private affairs should be dragged into the limelight?"

"They will not be unless they prove to be relevant to the death of George Barton."

"I see. You are suggesting that I first made love to his wife, and then murdered him?"

"Come, Mr. Farraday, I'll be frank with you. You and Mrs. Barton were very close friends—you parted by your wish, not the lady's. She was proposing, as this letter shows, to make trouble. Very conveniently, she died."

"She committed suicide. I dare say I may have been partly to blame. I may reproach myself, but it is no concern of the law's."

"It may have been suicide—it may not. George Barton thought not. He started to investigate—and he died. The sequence is rather suggestive."

"I do not see why you should—well, pitch on me."

"You admit that Mrs. Barton's death came at a very convenient moment for you? A scandal, Mr. Farraday, would have been highly prejudicial to your career."

"There would have been no scandal. Mrs. Barton would have seen reason."

"I wonder! Did your wife know about this affair, Mr. Farraday?"

"Certainly not."

"You are quite sure of that statement?"

"Yes, I am. My wife has no idea that there was anything but friendship between myself and Mrs. Barton. I hope she will never learn otherwise."

"Is your wife a jealous woman, Mr. Farraday?"

"Not at all. She has never displayed the least jealousy where I am concerned. She is far too sensible."

The Inspector did not comment on that. Instead he said, "Have you at any time in the past year had cyanide in your possession, Mr. Farraday?"

"No."

"But you keep a supply of cyanide at your country property?"

"The gardener may. I know nothing about it."

"You have never purchased any yourself at a chemist's or for photography?"

"I know nothing of photography—and I repeat that I have never purchased cyanide."

Kemp pressed him a little further before he finally let him go.

To his subordinate he said thoughtfully, "He was very quick denying that his wife knew about his affair with the Barton woman. Why was that, I wonder?"

"Dare say he's in a funk in case she should get to hear of it, sir."

"That may be, but I should have thought he'd got the brains to see that if his wife was in ignorance, and would cut up rough, that gives him an additional motive for wanting to silence Rosemary Barton. To save his skin his line ought to have been that his wife more or less knew about the affair but was content to ignore it."

"I dare say he hadn't thought of that, sir."

Kemp shook his head. Stephen Farraday was not a fool. He had a clear and astute brain. And he had been passionately keen to impress on the Inspector that Sandra knew nothing.

"Well," said Kemp, "Colonel Race seems pleased with the line he's dug up and if he's right, the Farradays are out—both of them. I shall be glad if they are. I like this chap. And personally I don't think he's a murderer."

Opening the door of their sitting room, Stephen said, "Sandra?"

She came to him out of the darkness, suddenly holding him, her hands on his shoulders. "Stephen?"

"Why are you all in the dark?"

"I couldn't bear the light. Tell me."

He said, "They know."

"About Rosemary?"

"Yes."

"And what do they think?"

"They see, of course, that I have a motive . . . Oh, my darling, see what I've dragged you into. It's all my fault. If only I'd cut loose after Rosemary's death—gone away —left you free—so that at any rate *you* shouldn't be mixed up in all this horrible business."

"No, not that . . . Never leave me . . . never leave me."

She clung to him—she was crying, the tears coursing down her cheeks. He felt her shudder.

"You're my life, Stephen, all my life—never leave me . . ."

"Do you care so much, Sandra? I never knew . . ."

"I didn't want you to know. But now—"

"Yes, now . . . We're in this together, Sandra . . . we'll face it together . . . whatever comes, together!"

Strength came to them as they stood there, clasped together in the darkness.

Sandra said with determination, "This shall *not* wreck our lives! It shall not. It shall *not!*"

CHAPTER 10

ANTHONY BROWNE looked at the card the little page was holding out to him.

He frowned, then shrugged his shoulders. He said to the boy, "All right, show him up."

When Colonel Race came in, Anthony was standing by the window with the bright sun striking obliquely over his shoulder.

He saw a tall, soldierly man with a lined bronze face and iron-grey hair—a man whom he had seen before, but not for some years, and a man whom he knew a good deal about.

Race saw a dark, graceful figure and the outline of a well-shaped head. A pleasant indolent voice said, "Colonel Race? You were a friend of George Barton's, I know. He talked about you on that last evening. Have a cigarette?"

"Thank you. I will."

Anthony said as he held a match, "You were the expected guest that night who did not turn up—just as well for you."

"You are wrong there. That empty place was not for me."

Anthony's eyebrows went up.

"Really? Barton said—"

Race cut in.

"George Barton may have said so. His plans were quite different. That chair, Mr. Browne, was intended to be occupied, when the lights went down, by an actress called Chloe West."

Anthony stared.

"Chloe West? Never heard of her. Who is she?"

"A young actress not very well known but who possesses a certain superficial resemblance to Rosemary Barton."

163

Anthony whistled.

"I begin to see."

"She had been given a photograph of Rosemary so that she could copy the style of headdress and she also had the dress which Rosemary wore the night she died."

"So that was George's plan? Up go the lights—hey, presto, gasps of supernatural dread! *Rosemary has come back*. The guilty party gasps out, 'It's true—it's true—I dunnit!' " He paused and added, "Rotten—even for an ass like poor old George."

"I'm not sure I understand you."

Anthony grinned.

"Oh, come now, sir—a hardened criminal isn't going to behave like a hysterical schoolgirl. If somebody poisoned Rosemary Barton in cold blood, and was preparing to administer the same fatal dose of cyanide to George Barton, that person had a certain amount of nerve. It would take more than an actress dressed up as Rosemary to make him or her spill the beans."

"Macbeth, remember, a decidedly hardened criminal, went to pieces when he saw the ghost of Banquo at the feast."

"Ah, but what Macbeth saw really *was* a ghost! It wasn't a ham actor wearing Banquo's duds! I'm prepared to admit that a real ghost might bring its own atmosphere from another world. In fact, I am willing to admit that I believe in ghosts—have believed in them for the last six months—one ghost in particular."

"Really—and whose ghost is that?"

"Rosemary Barton's. You can laugh if you like. I've not seen her—but I've felt her presence. For some reason or other Rosemary, poor soul, can't stay dead."

"I could suggest a reason."

"Because she was murdered?"

"To put it in another idiom, because she was bumped off. *How about that, Mr. Tony Morelli?*"

There was a silence. Anthony sat down, chucked his cigarette into the grate and lighted another one.

Then he said, "How did you find out?"

"You admit that you are Tony Morelli?"

"I shouldn't dream of wasting time by denying it.

164

You've obviously cabled to America and got all the dope."

"And you admit that when Rosemary Barton discovered your identity you threatened to bump her off unless she held her tongue?"

"I did everything I could think of to scare her into holding her tongue," agreed Tony pleasantly.

A strange feeling stole over Colonel Race. This interview was not going as it should. He stared at the figure in front of him lounging back in its chair—and an odd sense of familiarity came to him.

"Shall I recapitulate what I know about you, Morelli?"

"It might be amusing."

"You were convicted in the States of attempted sabotage in the Ericson Airplane works and were sentenced to a term of imprisonment. After serving your sentence, you came out and the authorities lost sight of you. You were next heard of in London, staying at Claridge's and calling yourself Anthony Browne. There you scraped acquaintance with Lord Dewsbury and through him you met certain other prominent armaments manufacturers. You stayed in Lord Dewsbury's house and by means of your position as his guest you were shown things which you ought never to have seen! It is a curious coincidence, Morelli, that a trail of unaccountable accidents and some very near escapes from disaster on a large scale followed very closely after your visits to various important works and factories."

"Coincidences," said Anthony, "are certainly extraordinary things."

"Finally, after another lapse in time, you reappeared in London and renewed your acquaintance with Iris Marle, making excuses not to visit her home, so that her family should not realize how intimate you were becoming. Finally, you tried to induce her to marry you secretly."

"You know," said Anthony, "it's really extraordinary the way you have found out all these things—I don't mean the armaments business—I mean my threats to Rosemary, and the tender nothings I whispered to Iris. Surely those don't come within the province of M.I.5!"

Race looked sharply at him.

"You've a good deal to explain, Morelli."

"Not at all. Granted your facts are all correct, what of them? I've served my prison sentence. I've made some interesting friends. I've fallen in love with a very charming girl and am naturally impatient to marry her."

"So impatient that you would prefer the wedding to take place before her family have the chance of finding out anything about your antecedents. Iris Marle is a very rich young woman."

Anthony nodded his head agreeably.

"I know. When there's money, families are inclined to be abominably nosey. And Iris, you see, doesn't know anything about my murky past. Frankly, I'd rather she didn't."

"I'm afraid she is going to know all about it."

"A pity," said Anthony.

"Possibly you don't realize—"

Anthony cut in with a laugh.

"Oh! I can dot the i's and cross the t's. Rosemary Barton knew my criminal past, so I killed her. George Barton was growing suspicious of me, so I killed him! Now I'm after Iris's money! It's all very agreeable and it hangs together nicely, but you haven't a mite of proof."

Race looked at him attentively for some minutes. Then he got up.

"Everything I have said is true," he said. *"And it's all wrong."*

Anthony watched him narrowly.

"What's wrong?"

"You're wrong." Race walked slowly up and down the room. "It hung together all right until I saw you—but now I've seen you, *it won't do. You're not a crook.* And if you're not a crook, you're one of *our* kind. I'm right, aren't I?"

Anthony looked at him in silence while a smile slowly broadened on his face. Then he hummed softly under his breath, " 'For the Colonel's lady and Judy O'Grady are sisters under the skin.' Yes, funny how one knows one's own kind. That's why I've tried to avoid meeting you. I was afraid you'd spot me for what I am. It was important

166

then that nobody should know—important up to yesterday. Now, thank goodness, the balloon's gone up! We've swept our gang of International saboteurs into the net. I've been working on this assignment for three years. Frequenting certain meetings, agitating among workmen, getting myself the right reputation. Finally, it was fixed that I pulled an important job and got sentenced. The business had to be genuine if I was to establish my *bona fides*.

"When I came out, things began to move. Little by little I got further into the centre of things—a great International net run from Central Europe. It was as *their* agent I came to London and went to Claridge's. I had orders to get on friendly terms with Lord Dewsbury—that was my lay, the social butterfly! I got to know Rosemary Barton in my character of attractive young man about town. Suddenly, to my horror, I found that she knew I had been in prison in America as Tony Morelli. I was terrified for *her!* The people I was working with would have had her killed without a moment's hesitation if they had thought she knew that. I did my best to scare her into keeping her mouth shut, But I wasn't very hopeful. Rosemary was born to be indiscreet. I thought the best thing I could do was to sheer off—and then I saw Iris coming down a staircase, and I swore that after my job was done I would come back and marry her.

"When the active part of my work was over, I turned up again and got into touch with Iris, but I kept aloof from the house and her people for I knew they'd want to make inquiries about me and I had to keep under cover for a bit longer. But I got worried about her. She looked ill and afraid—and George Barton seemed to be behaving in a very odd fashion. I urged her to come away and marry me. Well, she refused. Perhaps she was right. And then I was roped in for this party. It was as we sat down to dinner that George mentioned *you* were to be there. I said rather quickly that I'd met a man I knew and might have to leave early. Actually I *had* seen a fellow I knew in America—Monkey Coleman—though he didn't remember me—but I really wanted to avoid meeting you. I was still on my job.

"You know what happened next—George died. I had nothing to do with his death or with Rosemary's. I don't know now who did kill them."

"Not even an idea?"

"It must have been either the waiter or one of the five people round the table. I don't think it was the waiter. It wasn't me and it wasn't Iris. It could have been Sandra Farraday or it could have been Stephen Farraday, or it could have been both of them together. But the best bet, in my opinion, is Ruth Lessing."

"Have you anything to support that belief?"

"No. She seems to me the most likely person—but I don't see in the least how she did it! In both tragedies she was so placed at the table that it would be practically impossible for her to tamper with the champagne glass—and the more I think over what happened the other night, the more it seems to me impossible that George could have been poisoned—and yet he was!" Anthony paused. "And there's another thing that gets me—have you found out who wrote those anonymous letters that started him on the track?"

Race shook his head.

"No. I thought I had—but I was wrong."

"Because the interesting thing is that it means that there is *someone, somewhere,* who knows that Rosemary was murdered, so that, unless you're careful—that person will be murdered next!"

CHAPTER 11

FROM information received over the telephone, Anthony knew that Lucilla Drake was going out at five o'clock to drink a cup of tea with a dear old friend. Allowing for possible contingencies (returning for a purse, determination after all to take an umbrella just in case, and last minute chats on the doorstep), Anthony timed his own arrival at Elvaston Square at precisely twenty-five minutes past five. It was Iris he wanted to see, not her aunt. And, by all accounts, once shown into Lucilla's presence, he would have had very little chance of uninterrupted conversation with his lady.

He was told by the parlourmaid (a girl lacking the impudent polish of Betty Archdale) that Miss Iris had just come in and was in the study.

Anthony said with a smile, "Don't bother. I'll find my way," and went past her and along to the study door.

Iris spun round at his entrance with a nervous start.

"Oh, it's you."

He came over to her swiftly.

"What's the matter, darling?"

"Nothing." She paused, then said quickly, "Nothing. Only I was nearly run over. Oh, my own fault; I expect I was thinking so hard and mooning across the road without looking, and the car came tearing round a corner and just missed me."

He gave her a gentle little shake.

"You mustn't do that sort of thing, Iris. I'm worried about you—oh! not about your miraculous escape from under the wheels of a car, but about the reason that lets you moon about in the midst of traffic. What is it, darling? There's something special, isn't there?"

She nodded. Her eyes, raised mournfully to his, were large and dark with fear. He recognized their message even before she said very low and quick, *"I'm afraid."*

Anthony recovered his calm, smiling poise. He sat down beside Iris on a wide settee.

"Come on," he said, "let's have it."

"I don't think I want to tell you, Anthony."

"Now then, funny, don't be like the heroines of third-rate thrillers who start in the very first chapter by having something they can't possible tell for no real reason except to gump up the hero and make the book spin itself out for another fifty thousand words."

She gave a faint, pale smile.

"I want to tell you, Anthony, but I don't know what you'd think—I don't know if you'd believe—"

Anthony raised a hand and began to check off the fingers.

"One, an illegitimate baby. Two, a blackmailing lover. Three—"

She interrupted him indignantly.

"Of course not. Nothing of *that* kind."

"You relieve my mind," said Anthony. "Come on, little idiot."

Iris's face clouded over again.

"It's nothing to laugh at. It's—it's about the other night."

"Yes?" His voice sharpened.

Iris said, "You were at the inquest this morning—you heard—"

She paused.

"Very little," said Anthony. "The police surgeon being technical about the cyanides generally and the effect of potassium cyanide on George, and the police evidence as given by that first inspector; not Kemp, the one with the smart moustache who arrived first at the Luxembourg and took charge. Identification of the body by George's chief clerk. The inquest was then adjourned for a week by a properly docile coroner."

"It's the Inspector I mean," said Iris. "He described finding a small paper packet under the table containing traces of potassium cyanide."

Anthony looked interested.

"Yes. Obviously whoever slipped that stuff into George's glass just dropped the paper that had contained it under the table. Simplest thing to do. Couldn't risk having it found on him—or her."

To his surprise Iris began to tremble violently.

"Oh, no, Anthony. Oh, no, it wasn't like that."

"What do you mean, darling? What do you know about it?"

Iris said, *"I dropped that packet under the table."*

He turned astonished eyes upon her.

"Listen, Anthony. You remember how George drank off that champagne and then it happened?"

He nodded.

"It was awful—like a bad dream. Coming just when everything had seemed to be all right. I mean that, after the cabaret, when the lights went up—I felt so relieved.

170

Because it was *then,* you know, that we found Rosemary dead—and somehow, I don't know why, I felt I'd see it all happen again . . . I felt she was there, dead, at the table . . ."

"Darling . . ."

"Oh, I know. It was just nerves. But anyway, there we were, and there was nothing awful and suddenly it seemed the whole thing was really done with at last and one could —I don't know how to explain it—*begin again.* And so I danced with George and really felt I was enjoying myself at last, and we came back to the table. And then George suddenly talked about Rosemary and asked us to drink to her memory and then *he* died and all the nightmare had come back.

"I just felt paralyzed I think. I stood there, shaking. You came round to look at him, and I moved back a little, and the waiters came and someone asked for a doctor. And all the time I was standing there frozen. Then suddenly a big lump came in my throat and tears began to run down my cheeks and I jerked open my bag to get my handkerchief. I just fumbled in it, not seeing properly, and got out my handkerchief—a folded stiff bit of white paper, like the kind you get powders in from the chemist. Only, you see, Anthony, *it hadn't been in my bag when I started from home.* I hadn't had anything like that! I'd put the things in myself when the bag was quite empty—a powder compact, a lipstick, my handkerchief, my evening comb in its case, and a shilling and a couple of sixpences. *Somebody had put that packet in my bag*—they must have done. And I remembered how they'd found a packet like that in Rosemary's bag after she died and how it had had cyanide in it. I was frightened, Anthony, I was horribly frightened. My fingers went limp and the packet fluttered down from the handkerchief under the table. I let it go. And I didn't say anything. I was too frightened. Somebody meant it to look as though I had killed George, and I *didn't.*"

Anthony gave vent to a long and prolonged whistle.

"And nobody saw you?" he said.

Iris hesitated.

"I'm not sure," she said slowly. "I believe Ruth noticed. But she was looking so dazed that I don't know whether she really *noticed*—or if she was just staring at me blankly."

Anthony gave another whistle.

"This," he remarked, "is a pretty kettle of fish."

Iris said, "It got worse and worse. I've been so afraid they'd find out."

"Why weren't your fingerprints on it, I wonder? The first thing they'd do would be to fingerprint it."

"I suppose it was because I was holding it through the handkerchief."

Anthony nodded.

"Yes, you had luck there."

"But who could have put it in my bag? I had my bag with me all the evening."

"That's not so impossible as you think. When you went to dance after the cabaret, you left your bag on the table. Somebody may have tampered with it then. And there are the women. Could you get up and give me an imitation of just how a woman behaves in the ladies' cloakroom? It's the sort of thing I wouldn't know. Do you congregate and chat or do you drift off to different mirrors?"

Iris considered.

"We all went to the same table—a great long glasstopped one. And we put our bags down and looked at our faces, you know."

"Actually I don't. Go on."

"Ruth powdered her nose and Sandra patted her hair and pushed a hairpin in and I took off my fox cape and gave it to the woman and then I saw I'd got some dirt on my hand—a smear of mud, and I went over to the washbasins."

"Leaving your bag on the glass table?"

"Yes. And I washed my hands. Ruth was still fixing her face I think and Sandra went and gave up her cloak and then she went back to the glass and Ruth came and washed her hands and I went back to the table and just fixed my hair a little."

"So either of those two could have put something in your bag without your seeing?"

"Yes, but the packet was empty. So surely it must have een put in *after* George's champagne had been poioned. Anyway, I can't believe either Ruth or Sandra ould do such a thing."

"You think too highly of people. Sandra is the kind of othic creature who would have burned her enemies at e stake in the Middle Ages—and Ruth would make e most devastatingly practical poisoner that ever epped this earth."

"If it was Ruth, why didn't she say she saw me drop ?"

"You have me there. If Ruth deliberately planted cyaide on you, she'd take jolly good care you didn't get rid f it. So it looks as though it wasn't Ruth. In fact, the aiter is far and away the best bet. The waiter, the aiter! If only we had a strange waiter, a peculiar waiter, waiter hired for that evening only. But instead, we have iuseppe and Pierre and they just don't fit . . ."

Iris sighed.

"I'm glad I've told you. No one will ever know now, ill they? Only you and I?"

Anthony looked at her with a rather embarrassed exression.

"It's not going to be just like that, Iris. In fact you're oming with me now in a taxi to old man Kemp. We can't eep this under our hats."

"Oh, no, Anthony. They'll think I killed George."

"They'll certainly think so if they find out later that ou sat tight and said nothing about all this! Your explaation will then sound extremely thin. If you volunteer now, there's a likelihood of its being believed."

"Please, Anthony."

"Look here, Iris, you're in a tight place. But apart from nything else, there's such a thing as *truth*. You can't lay safe and take care of your own skin when it's a quesion of justice."

"Oh, Anthony, must you be so grand?"

"That," said Anthony, "was a very shrewd blow! But ll the same we're going to Kemp! Now!"

Unwillingly she came with him out into the hall. Her

coat was lying tossed on a chair and he took it and he
it out for her to put on.

There was both mutiny and fear in her eyes, but A
thony showed no sign of relenting. He said, "We'll pic
up a taxi at the end of the Square."

As they went towards the hall door the bell was presse
and they heard it ringing in the basement below.

Iris gave an exclamation.

"I forgot. It's Ruth. She was coming here when she le
the office to settle about the funeral arrangements. It
to be the day after tomorow. I thought we could sett
things better while Aunt Lucilla was out. She does con
fuse things so."

Anthony stepped forward and opened the door, fore
stalling the parlourmaid who came running up the stair
from below.

"It's all right, Evans," said Iris, and the girl wen
down again.

Ruth was looking tired and rather dishevelled. Sh
was carrying a large-sized attaché case.

"I'm sorry I'm late, but the tube was so terrib
crowded tonight and then I had to wait for three buse
and not a taxi in sight."

It was, thought Anthony, unlike the efficient Ruth t
apologize. Another sign that George's death had suc
ceeded in shattering that almost unhuman efficiency.

Iris said, "I can't come with you now, Anthony. Rut
and I must settle things."

Anthony said firmly, "I'm afraid this is more importan
. . . I'm awfully sorry, Miss Lessing, to drag Iris off lik
this, but it really *is* important."

Ruth said quickly, "That's quite all right, Mr. Browne
I can arrange everything with Mrs. Drake when sh
comes in." She smiled faintly. "I can really manage he
quite well, you know."

"I'm sure you could manage anyone, Miss Lessing,
said Anthony admiringly.

"Perhaps, Iris, if you can tell me any special points?"

"There aren't any. I suggested our arranging this to
gether simply because Aunt Lucilla changes her min
about everything every two minutes, and I thought

174

would be rather hard on you. You've had so much to do. But I really don't care what sort of funeral it is! Aunt Lucilla *likes* funerals, but I hate them. You've got to bury people, but I hate making a fuss about it. It can't matter to the people themselves. They've got away from it all. The dead don't come back."

Ruth did not answer, and Iris repeated with a strange defiant insistence, "The dead don't come back!"

"Come on," said Anthony, and pulled her out through the open door.

A cruising taxi was coming slowly along the Square. Anthony hailed it and helped Iris in.

"Tell me, beautiful," he said, after he had directed the driver to go to Scotland Yard, "who exactly did you feel was there in the hall when you found it so necessary to affirm that the dead are dead? Was it George or Rosemary?"

"Nobody! Nobody at all! I just hate funerals, I tell you." Anthony sighed.

"Definitely," he said, "I must be psychic!"

CHAPTER 12

THREE men sat at a small, round, marble-topped table.

Colonel Race and Chief Inspector Kemp were drinking cups of dark brown tea, rich in tannin. Anthony was drinking an English café's idea of a nice cup of coffee. It was not Anthony's idea, but he endured it for the sake of being admitted on equal terms to the other two men's conference.

Chief Inspector Kemp, having painstakingly verified Anthony's credentials, had consented to recognize him as a colleague.

"If you ask me," said the Chief Inspector, dropping several lumps of sugar into his black brew and stirring it painstakingly, "this case will never be brought to trial. We'll never get the evidence."

"You think not?" asked Race.

Kemp shook his head and took an approving sip of his tea.

"The only hope was to get evidence concerning the actual purchasing or handling of cyanide by one of those five. I've drawn a blank everywhere. It'll be one of those cases where you *know* who did it, and you can't ever prove it."

"So you know who did it?" Anthony regarded him with interest.

"Well, I'm pretty certain in my own mind. Lady Alexandra Farraday."

"So that's your bet," said Race. "Reasons?"

"You shall have 'em. I'd say she's the type that's madly jealous. And autocratic, too. Like that queen in history —Eleanor of Something, that followed the clue to Fair Rosamund's Bower and offered her the choice of a dagger or a cup of poison."

"Only in this case," said Anthony, "she didn't offer Fair Rosemary any choice."

Chief Inspector Kemp went on.

"Someone tips Mr. Barton off. He becomes suspicious —and I should say his suspicions were pretty definite. He wouldn't have gone as far as actually buying a house in the country unless he wanted to keep an eye on the Farradays. He must have made it pretty plain to her—harping on this party and urging them to come to it. She's not the kind to wait and see. Autocratic again, she finished him off! That, you may say, so far, is all theory and based on character. But I'll say that the *only* person who could have had any chance whatever of dropping something into Mr. Barton's glass just before he drank would be the lady on his right."

"And nobody saw her do it?" said Anthony.

"Quite. They might have—but they didn't. Say, if you like, she was pretty adroit."

"A positive conjuror."

Race coughed. He took out his pipe and began stuffing the bowl.

"Just one minor point. Granted Lady Alexandra is autocratic, jealous and passionately devoted to her husband,

176

granted that she'd not stick at murder, do you think she is the type to slip incriminating evidence into a girl's handbag? A perfectly innocent girl, mind, who had never harmed her in anyway? Is that in the Kidderminster tradition?"

Inspector Kemp squirmed uneasily in his seat and peered into his teacup.

"Women don't play cricket," he said, "if that's what you mean."

"Actually, a lot of them do," said Race, smiling. "But I'm glad to see you look uncomfortable."

Kemp escaped from his dilemma by turning to Anthony with an air of gracious patronage.

"By the way, Mr. Browne (I'll still call you that, if you don't mind), I want to say that I'm very much obliged to you for the prompt way you brought Miss Marle along this evening to tell that story of hers."

"I had to do it promptly," said Anthony. "If I'd waited I should probably not have brought her along at all."

"She didn't want to come, of course," said Colonel Race.

"She'd got the wind up badly, poor kid," said Anthony. "Quite natural, I think."

"Very natural," said the Inspector and poured himself out another cup of tea. Anthony took a gingerly sip of coffee.

"Well," said Kemp, "I think we relieved her mind—she went off home quite happily."

"After the funeral," said Anthony, "I hope she'll get away to the country for a bit. Twenty-four hours' peace and quiet away from Auntie Lucilla's non-stop tongue will do her good, I think."

"Aunt Lucilla's tongue has its uses," said Race.

"You're welcome to it," said Kemp. "Lucky I didn't think it necessary to have a shorthand report made when I took her statement. If I had, the poor fellow would have been in hospital with writer's cramp."

"Well," said Anthony. "I dare say you're right, Chief Inspector, in saying that the case will never come to trial —but that's a very unsatisfactory finish—and there's one thing we still don't know—who wrote those letters to George Barton telling him his wife was murdered? We haven't the least idea who that person is."

Race said, "Your suspicions still the same, Browne?"

"Ruth Lessing? Yes, I stick to her as my candidate. You told me that she admitted to you she was in love with George. Rosemary, by all accounts, was pretty poisonous to her. Say she saw suddenly a good chance of getting rid of Rosemary, and was fairly convinced that with Rosemary out of the way, she could marry George out of hand."

"I grant you all that," said Race. "I'll admit that Ruth Lessing has the calm, practical efficiency that can contemplate and carry out murder, and that she perhaps lacks that quality of pity which is essentially a product of imagination. Yes, I give you the first murder. But I simply can't see her committing the second one. I simply cannot see her panicking and poisoning the man she loved and wanted to marry! Another point that rules her out—why did she hold her tongue when she saw Iris throw the cyanide packet under the table?"

"Perhaps she didn't see her do it," suggested Anthony, rather doubtfully.

"I'm fairly sure she did," said Race. "When I was questioning her, I had the impression that she was keeping something back. And Iris Marle herself thought Ruth Lessing saw her."

"Come now, Colonel," said Kemp. "Let's have your 'spot.' You've got one, I suppose?"

"Out with it. Fair's fair. You've listened to ours—and raised objections."

Race's eyes went thoughtfully from Kemp's face to Anthony's and rested there.

Anthony's eyebrows rose.

"Don't say you still think I am the villain of the piece?"

Slowly Race shook his head.

"I can imagine no possible reason why you should kill George Barton. I think I know who did kill him—and Rosemary Barton, too."

"Who is it?"

Race said musingly, "Curious how we have all selected

women as suspects. I suspect a woman, too." He paused and said quietly, "I think the guilty person is Iris Marle."

With a crash Anthony pushed his chair back. For a moment his face went dark crimson—then with an effort, he regained command of himself. His voice, when he spoke, had a slight tremor but was deliberately as light and mocking as ever.

"By all means let us discuss the possibility," he said. "Why Iris Marle? And if so, why should she, of her own accord, tell me about dropping the cyanide paper under the table?"

"Because," said Race, "she knew that Ruth Lessing had seen her do it."

Anthony considered the reply, his head on one side. Finally he nodded.

"Passed," he said. "Go on. Why did you suspect her in the first place?"

"Motive," said Race. "An enormous fortune had been left to Rosemary in which Iris was not to participate. For all we know she may have struggled for years with a sense of unfairness. She was aware that if Rosemary died childless, all that money came to her. And Rosemary was depressed, unhappy, run down after 'flu,' just the mood when a verdict of suicide would be accepted without question."

"That's right, make the girl out a monster!" said Anthony.

"Not a monster," said Race. "There is another reason why I suspected her—a far-fetched one, it may seem to you—Victor Drake."

"Victor Drake?" Anthony stared.

"Bad blood. You see, I didn't listen to Lucilla Drake for nothing. I know all about the Marle family. Victor Drake—not so much weak as positively evil. His mother, feeble in intellect and incapable of concentration. Hector Marle, weak, vicious, and a drunkard. Rosemary, emotionally unstable. A family history of weakness, vice and instability. Predisposing causes."

Anthony lit a cigarette. His hands trembled.

"Don't you believe that there may be a sound blossom on a weak or even a bad stock?"

"Of course there may. But I am not sure that Iris Marle *is* a sound blossom."

"And my word doesn't count," said Anthony slowly, "because I'm in love with her. George showed her those letters, and she got in a funk and killed him? That's how it goes on, is it?"

"Yes. Panic *would* obtain in her case."

"And how did she get the stuff into George's champagne glass?"

"That, I confess, I do not know."

"I'm thankful there's something you don't know." Anthony tilted his chair back and then forward. His eyes were angry and dangerous. "You've got a nerve saying all this to me."

Race replied quietly, "I know. But I considered it had to be said."

Kemp watched them both with interest, but he did not speak. He stirred his tea round and round absent-mindedly.

"Very well." Anthony sat upright. "Things have changed. It's no longer a question of sitting round a table, drinking disgusting fluids, and airing academic theories. This case has *got* to be solved. We've *got* to resolve all the difficulties and get at the truth. That's got to be my job—and I'll do it somehow. I've got to hammer at the things we don't know—because when we do know them, the whole thing will be clear.

"I'll re-state the problem. Who knew that Rosemary had been murdered? Who wrote to George telling him so? Why did they write to him?

"And now the murders themselves. Wash out the first one. It's too long ago, and we don't know exactly what happened. But the second murder took place in front of my eyes. I *saw* it happen. Therefore, I ought to know *how* it happened. The ideal time to put the cyanide in George's glass was during the cabaret—but it couldn't have been put in then because he drank from his glass immediately afterwards. I *saw* him drink. After he drank nobody put anything in his glass. Nobody touched his glass, nevertheless, next time he drank, it was full of cyanide. He *couldn't* have been poisoned—but he was! There was cyanide in his glass—*but nobody could have put it there!* Are we getting on?"

"No," said Chief Inspector Kemp.

"Yes," said Anthony. "The thing has now entered into the realm of a conjuring trick. Or a spirit manifestation. I will now outline my psychic theory. Whilst we were dancing, the ghost of Rosemary hovers near George's glass and drops in some cleverly materialized cyanide— any spirit can make cyanide out of ectoplasm. George comes back and drinks her health and—oh, *Lord!*"

The other two stared curiously at him. His hands were holding his head. He rocked to and fro in apparent mental agony. He said, "That's it . . . that's it . . . the bag . . . the waiter . . ."

"The waiter?" Kemp was alert

Anthony shook his head.

"No, no. I don't mean what you mean. I did think once that what we needed was a waiter who was not a waiter before. Instead, we had a waiter who had always been a waiter—and a little waiter who was of the Royal Line of waiters—a cherubic waiter—a waiter above suspicion. And he's still above suspicion—but he played his part! Oh, Lord, yes, he played a star part."

He stared at them.

"Don't you see it? A waiter could have poisoned the champagne but the waiter didn't. Nobody touched George's glass, but George was poisoned. *A,* indefinite article. *The,* definite article. George's glass! George! Two separate things. And the money—lots and lots of money! And who knows—perhaps love as well? Don't look at me as though I'm mad. Come on, I'll show you."

Thrusting his chair back he sprang to his feet and caught Kemp by the arm.

"Come with me."

Kemp cast a regretful glance at his half-full cup.

"Got to pay," he muttered.

"No, no, we'll be back in a moment. Come on. I must show you outside. Come on, Race."

Pushing the table aside, he swept them away with him to the vestibule.

"You see that telephone box there?"

"Yes."

Anthony felt in his pockets.

"Damn, I haven't got twopence. Never mind. On second thought, I'd rather not do it that way. Come back."

They went back into the café, Kemp first, Race following with Anthony's hand on his arm.

Kemp had a frown on his face as he sat down and picked up his pipe. He blew down it carefully and began to operate on it with a hairpin which he brought out of his waistcoat pocket.

Race was frowning at Anthony with a puzzled face. He leaned back and picked up his cup, draining the remaining fluid in it.

"Damn," he said violently. "It's got sugar in it!"

He looked across the table to meet Anthony's slowly widening smile.

"Hullo," said Kemp, as he took a sip from his cup. "What the hell's this?"

"Coffee," said Anthony. "And I don't think you'll like it. I didn't."

CHAPTER 13

ANTHONY had the pleasure of seeing instant comprehension flash into the eyes of both his companions.

His satisfaction was short-lived, for another thought struck him with the force of a physical blow. He ejaculated out loud, "My God—that *car!*"

He sprang up.

"Fool that I was—idiot! She told me that a car had nearly run her down—and I hardly listened. Come on, quick!"

Kemp said, "She said she was going straight home when she left the Yard."

"Yes. Why didn't I go with her?"

"Who's at the house?" asked Race.

"Ruth Lessing was there, waiting for Mrs. Drake. It's possible that they're both discussing the funeral still!"

"Discussing everything else as well, if I know Mrs. Drake," said Race. He added abruptly, "Has Iris Marle any other relations?"

"Not that I know of."

"I think I see the direction in which your thoughts, ideas, are leading you. But—is it physically possible?"

"I think so. Consider for yourself how much has been taken for granted *on one person's word.*"

Kemp was paying the check. The three men hurried out as Kemp said, "You think the danger is acute? To Miss Marle?"

"Yes, I do."

Anthony swore under his breath and hailed a taxi. The three men got in and the driver was told to go to Elvaston Square as quickly as possible.

Kemp said slowly, "I've only got the general idea as yet. It washes the Farradays right out."

"Yes."

"Thank goodness for that. But surely there wouldn't be another attempt—so soon?"

"The sooner the better," said Race. "Before there's any chance of our minds running on the right track. Third time lucky—that will be the idea." He added, "Iris Marle told me, in front of Mrs. Drake, that she would marry you as soon as you wanted her to."

They spoke in spasmodic jerks, for the taxi driver was taking their directions literally and was hurtling round corners and cutting through traffic with immense enthusiasm.

Turning with a final spurt into Elvaston Square, he drew up with a terrific jerk in front of the house.

Elvaston Square had never looked more peaceful.

Anthony, with an effort regaining his usual cool manner, murmured, "Quite like the movies. Makes one feel rather a fool, somehow."

But he was on the top step ringing the bell while Race paid off the taxi and Kemp followed up the steps.

The parlourmaid opened the door.

Anthony said sharply, "Has Miss Iris got back?"

Evans looked a little surprised.

"Oh, yes sir. She came in half an hour ago."

Anthony breathed a sigh of relief. Everything in th[e] house was so calm and normal that he felt ashamed o[f] his recent melodramatic fears.

"Where is she?"

"I expect she's in the drawing-room with Mrs. Drake."

Anthony nodded and took the stairs in easy stride[s] Race and Kemp close beside him.

In the drawing-room, placid under its shaded electri[c] lights, Lucilla Drake was hunting through the pigeo[n] holes of the desk with the hopeful absorption of a terrie[r] and murmuring audibly, "Dear, dear, now where *did* [I] put Mrs. Marsham's letter? Now let me see . . ."

"Where's Iris?" demanded Anthony abruptly.

Lucilla turned and stared.

"Iris? She—I beg your pardon!" She drew herself u[p] "May I ask who you *are?*"

Race came forward from behind him and Lucilla's fac[e] cleared. She did not yet see Chief Inspector Kemp wh[o] was the third to enter the room.

"Oh, dear, Colonel Race! How kind of you to com[e] But I do wish you could have been here a little earlier— I *should* have liked to consult you about the funeral a[r]rangements—a man's advice, so valuable—and really [I] was feeling so upset, as I said to Miss Lessing, that reall[y] I couldn't even *think*—and I must say that Miss Lessin[g] was really very sympathetic for once and offered to d[o] everything she could to take the burden off my shoulder[s] —only, as she put it very reasonably, naturally *I* should b[e] the person most likely to know what were George's fa[a]vourite hymns—not that I actually *did*, because I'[m] afraid George didn't very often go to church—but na[t]urally, as a clergyman's wife—I mean widow—I do kno[w] what is *suitable*—"

Race took advantage of a momentary pause to slip i[n] his question, "Where is Miss Marle?"

"Iris? She came in some time ago. She said she had [a] headache and was going straight up to her room. You[ng] girls, you know, do not seem to me to have very muc[h] stamina nowadays—they don't eat enough spinach—an[d]

184

he seems positively to dislike talking about the funeral arrangements, but after all, *someone* has to do these things—and one does want to feel that everything has been done for the best, and proper respect shown to the dead— not that I have ever thought motor hearses really *reverent* —if you know what I mean—not like horses with their long black tails—but, of course, I said at once that it was quite all right and Ruth—I called her Ruth and not Miss Lessing—and I were managing splendidly, and she could leave everything to us."

Kemp asked, "Miss Lessing has gone?"

As the flow went on, Anthony edged gently out of the door. He had left the room before Lucilla, suddenly interrupting her narrative, paused to say, "Who *was* that young man who came with you? I didn't realize at first that *you* had brought him. I thought possibly he might have been one of those dreadful reporters. We have had such *trouble* with them."

Anthony was running lightly up the stairs. Hearing footsteps behind him, he turned his head, and grinned at Chief Inspector Kemp.

"You deserted, too? Poor old Race!"

Kemp muttered, "He does these things so nicely. I'm not popular in that quarter."

They were on the second floor and just preparing to start up the third when Anthony heard a light footstep descending. He pulled Kemp inside an adjacent bathroom door.

The footsteps went on down the stairs.

Anthony emerged and ran up the next flight of stairs. Iris's room, he knew, was the small one at the back. He tapped lightly on the door.

"Hi—Iris." There was no reply—and he knocked and called again. Then he tried the handle but found the door locked.

With real urgency now he beat upon it.

"Iris—Iris—"

After a second or two, he stopped and glanced down. He was standing on one of those woolly, old-fashioned rugs made to fit outside doors to obviate draughts. This one was close up against the door. Anthony kicked it

away. The space under the door at the bottom was qui
wide—sometime, he deduced, it had been cut to clear
fitted carpet instead of stained boards.

He stooped to the keyhole but could see nothing, b
suddenly he raised his head and sniffed. Then he l
down flat and pressed his nose against the crack under t
door.

Springing up, he shouted, "Kemp!"

There was no sign of the Chief Inspector. Anthon
shouted again.

It was Colonel Race, however, who came running u
the stairs. Anthony gave him no chance to speak. H
said, "Gas—pouring out! We'll have to break the do
down."

Race had a powerful physique. He and Anthony ma
short shrift of the obstacle. With a splintering, crackin
noise, the lock gave.

They fell back for a moment, then Race said, "She
there by the fireplace. I'll dash in and break the windov
You get her."

Iris Marle was lying by the gas fire—her mouth an
nose lying on the wide open gas jet.

A minute or two later, choking and spluttering, A
thony and Race laid the unconscious girl on the landi
floor in the draught of the passage window.

Race said, "I'll work on her. You get a doctor quic
ly."

Anthony swung down the stairs. Race called after hi
"Don't worry. I think she'll be all right. We got here
time."

In the hall Anthony dialled and spoke into the mout
piece, hampered by a background of exclamations fro
Lucilla Drake.

He turned at last from the telephone to say with a si
of relief, "Caught him. He lives just across the Squar
He'll be here in a couple of minutes."

"—but I must know what has *happened!* Is Iris ill
It was a final wail from Lucilla.

Anthony said, "She was in her room. Door locke
Her head in the gas fire and the gas full on."

"Iris?" Mrs. Drake gave a piercing shriek. "Iris has committed *suicide?* I can't believe it. I *don't* believe it!"

A faint ghost of Anthony's grin returned to him.

"You don't need to believe it," he said. "It isn't true."

CHAPTER 14

"AND NOW please, Tony, will you tell me all about it?"

Iris was lying on a sofa, and the valiant November sunshine was making a brave show outside the windows of Little Priors.

Anthony looked across at Colonel Race who was sitting on the window sill, and grinned engagingly.

"I don't mind admitting, Iris, that I've been waiting for this moment. If I don't soon explain to someone how clever I've been, I shall burst. There will be no modesty in this recital. It will be shameless blowing of my own trumpet with suitable pauses to enable you to say 'Anthony, how clever of you' or 'Tony, how wonderful' or some phrase of a like nature. Ahem! the performance will now begin. Here we go:

"The thing, as a whole, *looked* simple enough. What I mean is, that it looked like a clear case of cause and effect. Rosemary's death, accepted at the time as suicide, was not suicide. George became suspicious, started investigating, was presumably getting near the truth, and before he could unmask the murderer was, in his turn, murdered. The sequence, if I may put it that way, seems perfectly clear.

"But almost at once we came across some apparent contradictions. Such as: A. George could not be poisoned. B. George *was* poisoned. And: A. Nobody touched George's glass. B. George's glass was tampered with.

"Actually, I was overlooking a very significant fact—the varied use of the possessive case. George's ear is George's ear indisputably because it is attached to his head and cannot be removed without a surgical opera-

187

tion! But when I come to George's glass, or George's tea
cup, I being to realize that I mean something very vagu
indeed. All I actually mean is the glass or cup out o
which George has lately been drinking—and which ha
nothing to distinguish it from several other cups an
glasses of the same pattern.

"To illustrate this, I tried an experiment. Race wa
drinking tea without sugar, Kemp was drinking tea wit
sugar, and I was drinking coffee. In appearance the thre
fluids were of much the same colour. We were sittin
round a small, marble-topped table among several othe
round, marble-topped tables. On the pretext of an urger
brain wave I urged the other two out of their seats an
out into the vestibule, pushing the chairs aside as we wen
and also managing to move Kemp's pipe which was ly
ing by his plate to a similar position by my plate but with
out letting him see me do it. As soon as we were outside
made an excuse and we returned, Kemp slightly ahead
He pulled the chair to the table and sat down opposit
the plate that was marked by the pipe he had left behin
him. Race sat on his right as before and I on his left—
but mark what had happened—a new A. and B. contra
diction! A. Kemp's cup has sugared tea in it. B. Kemp'
cup has coffee in it. Two conflicting statements that *can
not* both be true—but they *are* both true. The mis
leading term is *Kemp's cup*. Kemp's cup when he *left* th
table and Kemp's cup when he *returned* to the table ar
not the same.

"And that, Iris, *is what happened at the Luxembour
that night.* After the cabaret, when you all went to danc
you dropped your bag. A waiter picked it up—not *th
waiter, the waiter attending on that table who knew jus
where you had been sitting—but *a* waiter, an anxiou
hurried little waiter with everybody bullying him, runnin
along with a sauce, and who quickly stooped, picked u
the bag and placed it by a plate—actually by the plat
one plate to the left of where you had been sitting. Yo
and George came back first and you went, without
thought, straight to the place marked by your bag—jus
as Kemp did to the place marked by his pipe. Georg
sat down in what he thought to be his place, on your righ

188

nd when he proposed his toast in memory of Rose-
ary, he drank from what he thought was *his* glass but
as in reality *your* glass—the glass that can quite easily
ave been poisoned without needing a conjuring trick
• explain it, because the only person who did *not* drink
ter the cabaret, was necessarily the *person whose health
as being drunk!*

"Now go over the whole business again and the setup
entirely different! *You* are the intended victim, not
eorge! So it looks, doesn't it, as though George is being
ed. What, if things had not gone wrong, would have
en the story as the world would see it? A repetition of
e party a year ago—and a repetition of—suicide! Clear-
, people would say, a suicidal streak in that family! Bit
paper which has contained cyanide found in your bag.
lear case! Poor girl has been brooding over her sister's
ath. Very sad—but these rich girls are sometimes
ry neurotic!"

Iris interrupted him. She cried out, "But why should
yone want to kill me? Why? *Why?*"

"All that lovely money, angel! Money, money, money!
osemary's money went to you on her death. Now, sup-
se you were to die—unmarried. What would happen to
at money? The answer was it would go to your next
kin—to your aunt, Lucilla Drake. Now from all ac-
unts of the dear lady, I could hardly see Lucilla Drake
First Murderess. But is there anyone else who would
nefit? Yes, indeed. Victor Drake. If Lucilla has money,
will be exactly the same as Victor having it—Victor will
e to that! He has always been able to do what he likes
ith his mother. And there is nothing difficult about see-
g Victor as First Murderer. All along, from the very
art of the case, there have been references to Victor,
entions of Victor. He has been there in the offing, a shad-
vy, unsubstantial, evil figure."

"But Victor's in the Argentine! He's been in South
merica for over a year."

"Has he? We're coming now to what has been said to
the fundamental plot of every story. 'Girl meets boy!'
hen Victor met Ruth Lessing, this particular story
arted. He got hold of her. I think she must have fallen

189

for him pretty badly. Those quiet, level-headed, la[w]
abiding women are the kind that often fall for a re[al]
bad lot.

"Think a minute and you'll realize that all the eviden[ce]
for Victor's being in South America depends on Ruth['s]
word. None of it was verified because it was never a ma[de]
issue! *Ruth* said that she had seen Victor off on the *S[an]
Cristobal* before Rosemary's death! It was *Ruth* who su[g]-
gested putting a call through to Buenos Aires on the da[y]
of George's death—and later sacked the telephone g[irl]
who might have inadvertently let out that she did [not]
such thing.

"Of course, it's been easy to check up now! Vict[or]
Drake arrived in Rio by a boat leaving England the da[y]
after Rosemary's death. Ogilvie, in Buenos Aires, had [no]
telephone conversation with Ruth on the subject of Vict[or]
Drake on the day of George's death. *And Victor Dra[ke]
left Buenos Aires for New York some weeks ago.* Ea[sy]
enough for him to arrange for a cable to be sent in h[is]
name on a certain day—one of those well known cabl[es]
asking for money that seemed proof positive that he wa[s]
many thousands of miles away. Instead of which—"

"Yes, Anthony?"

"Instead of which," said Anthony, leading up to h[is]
climax with intense pleasure, "he was sitting at the ne[xt]
table to ours at the Luxembourg with a not so dum[b]
blonde!"

"Not that awful looking man?"

"A yellow, blotchy complexion and bloodshot eyes a[re]
easy things to assume, and they make a lot of differen[ce]
to a man. Actually, of our party, *I* was the only pers[on]
(apart from Ruth Lessing) who had ever seen Vict[or]
Drake—and I had never known him under *that name!* [In]
any case, I was sitting with my back to him. I did think [I]
recognized, in the cocktail lounge outside, as we cam[e]
in, a man I had known in my prison days—Monke[y]
Coleman. But as I was now leading a highly respectab[le]
life, I was not too anxious that he should recognize me. [I]
never for one moment suspected that Monkey Colema[n]
had had anything to do with the crime—much less th[at]
he and Victor Drake were one and the same."

"But I don't see now how he did it."

Colonel Race took up the tale.

"In the easiest way in the world. During the cabaret he went out to telephone, passing our table. Drake had been an actor and he had been something more important—a *waiter*. To assume the make-up and play the part of Pedro Morales was child's play to an actor, but to move deftly round a table, with the step and gait of a waiter, filling up the champagne glasses, needed the definite knowledge and technique of a man who had actually *been* a waiter. A clumsy action or movement would have drawn your attention to him, but as a *bona fide* waiter none of you noticed or saw him. You were looking at the cabaret, not noticing that portion of the restaurant's furnishings—the waiter!"

Iris said, in a hesitating voice, "And Ruth?"

Anthony said, "It was Ruth, of course, who put the cyanide paper in your bag—probably in the cloakroom at the beginning of the evening. The same technique she had adopted a year ago—with Rosemary."

"I always thought it odd," said Iris, "that George hadn't told Ruth about those letters. He consulted her about everything."

Anthony gave a short laugh.

"Of course he told her—first thing. She knew he would. That's why she wrote them. Then she arranged all his 'plan' for him—having first got him well worked up. And so she had the stage set—all nicely arranged for suicide Number Two—and if George chose to believe that you had killed Rosemary and were committing suicide out of remorse or panic—well, that wouldn't make any difference to Ruth!"

"And to think I liked her—liked her very much! And actually wanted her to marry George."

"She'd probably have made him a very good wife, if she hadn't come across Victor," said Anthony. "Moral: every murderess was a nice girl once."

Iris shivered. "All that for money!"

"You innocent, money is what these things are done for! Victor certainly did it for money. Ruth partly for the money, partly for Victor, and partly, I think, because she hated Rosemary. Yes, she'd travelled a long way by the time she deliberately tried to run you down in a car and still further when she left Lucilla in the drawing room, banged the front door and then ran up to your bed room. What did she seem like? Excited at all?"

Iris considered.

"I don't think so. She just tapped on the door, came in, and said everything was fixed up and she hoped I was feeling all right. I said yes, I was just a bit tired. And then she picked up my big rubber-covered flashlight and said what a nice flashlight that was and after that I don't seem to remember anything."

"No, dear," said Anthony, "because she hit you a nice little crack, not too hard, on the back of the neck with your nice flashlight. Then she arranged you artistically by the gas fire, shut the windows tight, turned on the gas, went out, locking the door and passing the key underneath it, pushed the woolly mat close up against the crack so as to shut out any draught and tripped gently down the stairs. Kemp and I just got into the bathroom in time. I raced on up to you and Kemp followed Miss Ruth Lessing, unbeknownst, to where she had left that car parked—you know, I felt at the time there was something fishy and uncharacteristic about the way Ruth tried to force it on our minds that she had come by bus and tube!"

Iris gave a shudder.

"It's horrible—to think anyone was as determined to kill me as all that. Did she hate me, too, by then?"

"Oh, I shouldn't think so. But Miss Ruth Lessing is a very efficient young woman. She'd already been an accessory in two murders and she didn't fancy having risked her neck for nothing. I've no doubt Lucilla Drake bleated out your decision to marry me at a moment's notice, and in that case there was no time to lose. Once married, I should be your next of kin and not Lucilla."

"Poor Lucilla. I'm so terribly sorry for her."

"I think we all are. She's a harmless, kindly soul."

"Is he really arrested?"

Anthony looked at Race, who nodded and said, "This morning, when he landed in New York."

"Was he going to marry Ruth—afterwards?"

"That was Ruth's idea. I think she would have brought t off, too."

"Anthony—I don't think I like my money very much."

"All right, sweet—we'll do something noble with it if ou like. I've got enough money to live on—and to keep a wife in reasonable comfort. We'll give it all away if you ike—endow homes for children, or provide free tobacco or old men, or—how about a campaign for serving better coffee all over England?"

"I shall keep a little," said Iris. "So that if I ever wanted o, I could be grand and walk out and leave you."

"I don't think, Iris, that that is the right spirit to enter upon married life. And by the way, you didn't once say Tony, how wonderful' or 'Anthony, how clever of you!' "

Colonel Race smiled and got up.

"Going over to the Farradays' for tea," he explained. There was a faint twinkle in his eye as he said to Anthony, "Don't suppose you're coming?"

Anthony shook his head and Race went out of the room. He paused in the doorway to say, over his shoulder, "Good show."

"That," said Anthony as the door closed behind him, "denotes supreme British approval."

Iris asked in a calm voice, "He thought I'd done it, didn't he?"

"You mustn't hold that against him," said Anthony. "You see, he's known so many beautiful spies, all stealing secret formulas and wheedling secrets out of Major-generals, that it's soured his nature and warped his judgment. He thinks it's just got to be the beautiful girl in the case!"

"Why did you know I hadn't, Tony?"

"Just love, I suppose," said Anthony lightly.

Then his face changed, grew suddenly serious. He touched a little vase by Iris's side in which was a single sprig of grey-green with a mauve flower.

"What's that doing in flower at this time of year?"

"It does sometimes—just an odd sprig—if it's a mild autumn."

Anthony took it out of the glass and held it for a moment against his cheek. He half closed his eyes and saw rich chestnut hair, laughing blue eyes and a red passionate mouth. . . .

He said in a quiet conversational tone, "She's not around now any longer, is she?"

"Who do you mean?"

"You know who I mean. Rosemary. . . . I think she knew, Iris, that you were in danger."

He touched the sprig of fragrant green with his lips and threw it lightly out of the window.

"Good-bye, Rosemary, thank you. . . ."

Iris said softly, *"That's for remembrance. . . ."*

And more softly still, *"Pray, love, remember . . ."*